Table of Contents

Sunset Ghost and Second Chances

Barbara Baldwin

Print ISBNs

Amazon print 9780228631668
Ingram Spark 9780228631675
Barnes & Noble 9780228631682
BWL Print 9780228631699

BWL Publishing Inc.

Books we love to write ...
Authors around the world.

http://bwlpublishing.ca

Chapter 1
The House at the end of the Lane

I looked again at the directions I had scribbled on a note pad after talking to the realtor. This couldn't be right. Squinting through the windshield into the late afternoon sun, I tried to find the road he said would be there.

"Who ever heard of giving directions by counting telephone poles?" I muttered, even as I continued to count. "Eleven, twelve, thir—" I hit the brakes. Surely the dirt path on the left was not the road where he said to turn.

Cautiously I angled my car around telephone pole number thirteen and onto a path that was more undergrowth and sand than anything even remotely resembling a road. I slowed, picking up my cell phone from the seat beside me. Two bars. Great. If I did get stuck, chances were good I wouldn't even be able to call a tow truck.

I drove cautiously between outbreaks of wild roses whose long neglected branches reached out like octopus tentacles to snare me. I had almost decided I made a wrong turn when I saw a barely visible sign off to the side.

It swung at an odd angle from the post because one of the chains holding it was broken. I stopped the car and tilted my head so I could read it. It was the right realty; the huge red letters HN were a dead give-away. I grimaced as the belly of my Honda scraped bottom when I turned onto another roadway that may at one time have been gravel, then again maybe not.

I flipped off the air conditioner and opened the windows. The overhanging trees completely blocked the sun and the drop in temperature was unreal. Only a slight breeze filtered through the open space, but I could smell the salt air and knew; just knew, what I was looking for lay ahead. It had to be, because I was desperate.

I mentally slammed the door on thoughts I did not want to have. I wasn't desperate; I was on vacation. I was...

"Oh, my." I rounded a curve and the house came into view. It perched on a low hill, lush foliage surrounding it and so many wild sand rose bushes across the front that at first I didn't see the steps leading to the porch. Wood shingles and siding were weathered to gray. The hurricane shutters on each side of the windows had possibly been red or bright pink at one time but were now sun faded to a point of almost being colorless. As my gaze swept the exterior, I was happy to note that at least all the shutters were there, and the siding appeared to be sturdy.

I climbed out of the car, pulling my tee shirt away from my sweaty back. Coming to Cape Cod in July had sounded like such a great idea, but it wasn't just my sweat glands that were rebelling. My hair hadn't been the same since crossing onto the peninsula at Bournedale. The salt air and humidity did things to it that I didn't even want to think about, and I contemplated a hair cut—a very, very short hair cut.

Cape Cod really had nothing to do with my frizzy, blonde-streaked hair. I blamed my current, very confused state of mind on That Time; the eight months of numbing, heart wrenching pain I had endured before making a choice that would change my life forever.

"What do you want me to do?" My husband had asked when I had once again confronted him with his infidelity, and he had again denied any wrong doing.

"I want you to move out."

"I can't do that," he replied and I had actually felt a weight lift from my shoulders. I knew the choice was now mine.

A shiver raced down my spine even now, thinking of That Time. I had important decisions to make about the rest of my life, and I wanted to see if I could still write, an avocation I had been shamed into giving up.

The need to create happy endings again had been consuming me even as I struggled with my self esteem, mental and physical health, and the actual process of moving out of the home I had occupied for the past seven years. In my desperate flight, I left behind the majority of my possessions but what I wanted to leave behind—the hurt, betrayal and anger—somehow managed to climb into the packed car with me.

Maybe I could drown them in the ocean I heard crashing to shore on the other side of the house. I hurried around the side, careful where I walked because I wore sandals and the path—the wild rose strewn path—narrowed dangerously as I turned the corner. A dozen steps further and the overgrowth that blocked my view fell away, opening to a huge expanse of blue sky, even bluer water, and frothy waves that swept up then receded from a brown sugar beach. If ever there were a place of peace and forgiveness, this had to be it.

I sat right where I was, at the top of a small crest, and tried to soak it in. I closed my eyes and just listened, perhaps hoping for some inner voice to tell me this was the right choice; this was the place where I needed to be. I heard only the cycle of the waves, splashing then receding, but the longer I sat, the more I could feel my breathing and my heartbeat slowing to the same rhythm. The warmth of the day dried the tears on my cheeks. The ocean breeze swept across my shoulders in what I could only hope was a hug. Because I so needed a hug.

"Happy birthday to me," I whispered, watching the sky change colors as the sun sank behind me. I hadn't chosen to take my vacation at this particular time by accident. I knew I couldn't be alone in a small apartment on this particular day. I never thought I would be alone at this point in my life. Years ago, eons it seemed, I had thought by the time the kids were grown and on their own that it would be our time. That we would travel and explore, share and talk, listen and understand. But after one mid-life crisis too many on my husband's part, I knew the exploring would be done alone. So I had packed my car and driven to Cape Cod, hoping to escape my sorrow; wanting desperately—a word I seemed to use a lot lately—to find some inner peace and purpose for what remained of the rest of my life. In the serenity of a small town and away from everyone and everything I knew, I looked forward to discovering who I was and what I needed to be happy again.

Besides, I hoped the words would come so I could resume writing. Creative writing wasn't something I had ever been able to just sit down and do easily. It took something deep inside me to find the words to create a world and the characters to inhabit it. I hadn't realized how much I missed those imaginary people I created. Not until I stopped writing. Not until what I had created in the past was used as an excuse for inexcusable behavior and used to shame me. I was told not to share my writing of romance stories with people he knew because it was a reflection on him.

I was doing it again, I thought morosely. I constantly reminded myself I would not, could not, continue to dwell on the past and what would never be the same again. Now, forcing myself to my feet, I walked back to the house where a wide porch spanned the entire back side. A dilapidated hammock swung in the breeze until one end caught on a snag of wood from the porch railing. I cautiously placed a foot on the first step, stomped a little to make sure it would hold my weight, then stepped up to the second, repeating the process. Fantasies fluttered at the edge of my awareness of falling through the wood, getting stuck with no one to find me until my bones were bleached white from the summer sun.

Well, at least I hadn't totally forgotten how to create a fantasy.

I plugged the single key into the lock and turned, twisting the doorknob at the same time. As expected, the door squeaked and groaned as I pushed it open, reminding me of what an old wooden ship might sound like as it rolled about on a storm tossed sea. The interior was dark, and I left the door wide, hoping to shed a little light through the place. While the outside storm shutters weren't across the windows, inside blinds were drawn against the sun, fading out the furnishings.

The house felt lived in, although the realtor assured me no one had been in residence for many years. I felt a sensation of quiet watchfulness, as though someone waited just the other side of the hallway to welcome me. While I always considered I had a vivid imagination, which of course was a necessary requisite to any writing career, I didn't believe in ghosts or other-worldly creatures, so I wasn't sure exactly why I hesitated just inside the threshold.

"Hello?" I think I would have fainted if anyone had answered me, but still I felt I had to speak out loud.

The back door opened into the kitchen, and I walked across to the windows over the sink and slid up the blinds. What little sunlight left in the day filtered through dirty windows, but it gave me enough light to see the furnishings. The place was equipped with a stove and refrigerator; an old Formica table and chairs sat in the middle of a spacious room. A pantry-sized cupboard stood against the wall behind the door, and two archways opposite the sink opened to the other rooms.

I glanced quickly at my watch because the realtor had said the electricity wasn't on and I wanted to see the rest before it got dark. Actually, I wanted to be sure I could find my way back to town before it got dark, recalling the difficulty I had getting here. Peeking past the archway on the right I saw the living room; several pieces of furniture were draped with sheets. A dark wood, rolled-top desk and chair close to the front windows beckoned me, and I felt the urge to sit and just contemplate writing. Urges stirred within me even now, although I had no idea what I would write.

Don't force it. It will come when you're ready. It was my own advice, but also that of my writing friends, all of whom had experienced writer's block at one time or the other. But writer's block wasn't the same as... I let the thought go. I had to start letting go, I knew it. And I would. I knew that, too.

I retraced my steps to the kitchen and took the other archway, which opened to a short hall. Two closed doors faced each other. On the wall at the end was what looked like a framed picture, largely out of proportion for the amount of wall space. With no windows, it was darker here and all I could decern were splotches of dark color.

Time was running out, so I quickly opened one door to find a closet, and the opposite door led to a bathroom that had a claw-footed bathtub complete with a rust stain running from the faucet to the drain. The toilet had to be as old as modern plumbing would allow. The holding tank was elevated on pipes at least six feet above the floor, with a pull chain for the flushing mechanism. I shook my head in disbelief, and then smiled. At least it had indoor plumbing.

But where was the bedroom? I stepped back into the hall and looked both ways. Noticing a doorknob on the painting, I turned it and pulled. What I had thought was a wall turned out to be a door, as wide as the narrow hallway, almost like a secret passage.

Well, not so secret since there was a doorknob, but still, it could have been a secret passage at one time. I peered into the shadows, defining steps that led upward to the left. I hesitated.

Some light filtered down from above so I took a chance, using the narrow walls of the stairway to guide me. When my gaze came even with the floor, I knew this was the place where I wanted to spend the summer. If the price was right; if the stove and refrigerator worked, if I could find my way back here tomorrow. No ifs, I told myself as I climbed the rest of the way to a loft bedroom that spanned the entire length of the house. The sloped ceilings were high enough that I could walk comfortably without banging my head. There were porthole type windows low on the walls, several on each side that I hadn't noticed from the front of the house.

There were also two skylights with very little light coming through them. I realized any further exploration would have to wait until I actually rented the place. I made my way back down the stairs, cautiously closed the heavy door, thinking the painting may just have to go because I was sure that was the majority of weight I was pushing against.

When I locked up and climbed back into my car, I sat for a minute and looked at the house—a cottage really—and for the first time in over two months, a genuine smile touched my lips.

I can do this.

A last ray of sunlight glinted off a weathervane on the roof. I couldn't quite make out the figure that adorned it but realized that was just one more thing I had to look forward to discovering tomorrow.

* * *

I returned to the Fairbanks Inn where I had a reserved room. Freddie and Dennis weren't out back where I had met them yesterday when I arrived. They were two fun people and I hoped to catch up with them before the weekend was over. We had introduced ourselves the night before and enjoyed a glass of wine on the patio. They had come down from New York for the weekend and I felt our paths were destined to cross. Freddie had been married but he and his wife argued often and to the point that one day the police were called. He told me it had still taken him moving out five times before he finally decided it was over. Now at sixty years old and retired, he was having the best time of his life. His story made me hope I had something to look forward to in my later years.

I showered and changed, deciding not to mope around my room. It was a nice room, but small and just this side of being hot. Apparently air conditioning wasn't something people in Provincetown thought totally necessary. Instead of central air, there was a small window unit that rattled and shook when I flipped the switch to maximum cool. Grabbing my camera and some money, I walked the short distance to Commercial Street. It was only eight o'clock and there wasn't a lot of activity. Over the course of my stay, I had discovered things didn't liven up until around midnight.

Every touristy town probably had a street like Commercial Street. Bourbon Street in New Orleans and the River Walk in San Antonio came to mind—full of souvenir shops, bistros, outdoor cafes, bars and coffee shops. Couples who were out for an early dinner made me wish again for someone with whom I could share this adventure. Yes, I had come to write, and that was a solitary affair. Yet walking the beach, hearing area history and exploring the lighthouses were things meant to be shared.

I stood in line at Bubala's by the Bay, hoping for a seat outside. As evening approached, the air cooled and I thought perhaps an air conditioner wasn't a necessity, at least at night.

"How many?" the hostess asked when it was my turn.

"One."

She hesitated, as though I would tell her something different if she waited. Didn't anyone travel alone? Why ask, I thought as she led me to a table, you already came to that conclusion.

The table wiggled, one leg just a little shorter than the others, but being outside gave me time to observe people as they passed. As a writer, I was always looking for book characters, and here they were in the flesh. Guys and gals walked down the street that, although for cars, in the evening became a place to promenade.

Provincetown was rather liberal and uninhibited—sort of the San Francisco of the east coast. I watched as guys meandered by: old, young, tattooed, bald, skinny and stout. Many with partners and none seemed averse to showing their emotions. What a change from the life I had endured. The women who had partners were closer in age than the men, but all were just as confident in themselves and who they were. I wanted to find that confidence in myself again.

No one seemed in a hurry, and as acquaintances spied each other, they would hang over the low iron railing surrounding the outdoor patio and visit. Was Provincetown such a small place that everyone knew each other? Or did they come back year after year on vacation and renew friendships? If the first were the case, I was in trouble, because as a newbie, everyone would recognize I didn't belong. I couldn't even claim to be a "washashore", which is what they called residents who weren't born on the Cape. I wasn't technically even a resident.

I wondered how long it would take before I could go through a day when everything and everyone didn't remind me of what I no longer had.

"Bonnie?"

I turned at the sound of my name, thinking nobody in this town knew me, but I was wrong. "Freddie."

He wove his way through the tables to get to mine, Dennis not far behind.

"Can we join you? It's nuts out there—way too many people." This from Dennis, who waved his hand about negligently.

"You're from New York. How on earth can you think this is crowded?" I glanced beyond the low railing where plenty of people roamed the street, but it wasn't as though you couldn't walk.

"In New York, it's expected. I thought Provincetown would be much more laid back."

I shook my head. I guess reality was in the eyes of the beholder. "I would love for you to join me. I was just thinking...never mind. Sit down."

Throughout dinner and for several glasses of wine afterward, we talked and laughed and it felt good. I would most likely never see these two after their weekend was over, even though I planned to stay on the Cape for the summer. But it was nice to strike up a friendship for a short time.

"Freddie, what are you doing here? I thought you and Bob only came down late in September, after the invasion was over." A tall, good looking man slapped Freddie on the shoulder as he spoke. He glanced across at Dennis, then me. He had warm gray eyes and a very nice smile. His hair was longish and dark brown, just a little gray at the temples, a striking contrast to his deep tan.

"Hey, Robert," Freddie replied. "I thought you refused to reside here in the summer anymore with all the riff raff." I could tell by Freddie's smile they were good friends and liked to tease each other. "Oh, this is my friend, Dennis, from New York, and this is my new friend, Bonnie Keeler, from Kansas."

Robert nodded at Dennis but smiled at me. I put out my hand. "Very nice to meet a friend of Freddie's. I'm part of the invasion." I smiled to take any sting out of my words.

He laughed outright, a deep, incredibly robust laugh. "I apologize." He pulled the fourth chair out and sat beside me, making himself at home. "For years, P'town was small and bohemian and everyone knew everyone and we all got along. Then someone spilled the beans and let our secret out. Suddenly we were inundated with tourists—"

"Invaders?" I interrupted.

"Call them what you will. They made a difference in this town. Mostly good, of course, with the influx of new money and the need for more B&B's, hotels and businesses. We all benefit. And it's not like Sturgis with those crazy motorcycle fanatics and their raunchy parties. At least our returning couples and the events of Bear Week are done tastefully." He stopped long enough to take a sip of wine the waitress had brought him.

"So you'll take our money but you'd really prefer we not be here?" I asked.

Robert sighed dramatically. "I know. That sounds terribly paradoxical, doesn't it?"

My lips curved at both his mannerism and language.

Freddie's foot connected gently with my shin under the table. I looked at him as he ever so slightly inclined his head toward Robert. He raised a brow and smiled at me and like a thunderbolt out of the blue, I realized he was telling me Robert was an available male.

Oh, Lord, please. As I sat there with the cool ocean breeze fuzzing my hair, I realized how dormant my entire body, and especially my brain, had become over the years. I knew nothing about flirting. I hadn't even worn makeup to dinner.

"Bonnie's a writer," Freddie said, apparently trying to help out. "You should get her books for your shop."

"Really? What do you write?" Robert turned toward me, draping an arm over the back of my chair.

Knowing most men's reactions to the word erotica, I said instead, "Romance, ghost stories, and then to pay the bills I write grants and magazine articles."

His brows rose. "I'm impressed."

I hoped he would let the subject drop.

"What kind of romance?"

What did it matter if I told the truth? It wasn't like I'd see this guy again. I wasn't ashamed of what I wrote, even if my soon-to-be-ex-husband had tried to make me so.

"I started out with historical, and then wrote some time travel." I paused before adding, "Lately I've been writing contemporary erotica."

Robert raised his brow again. "Hot stuff?"

I blushed. I wasn't used to anyone asking so many questions about my writing. I wasn't used to talking about it at all—even the mundane aspects of setting or plot—because my husband hadn't been interested. He had only been interested in me not sharing it with the wives of his associates.

Robert was still watching me and it took a minute to remember his question. His direct gaze was inquisitive, interested, and teasing.

"My writing's not as hot as some authors, but yeah, there's plenty of sensuous, sexy lovemaking."

His face broke into a grin. "Nice!"

Chapter 2
A Beginning

"Where are you going?" Freddie asked the next morning when I came down for breakfast on the patio.

I dropped my bags next to the wall so they wouldn't be in anyone's way and helped myself to a cup of coffee.

"I have to find a place to live. My reservation here is done." I plopped in a chair beside him.

"You can stay with Dennis and me for the rest of the weekend."

I slanted a gaze his way.

"Well, at least you'd know you were safe." He grinned.

"You know, I think I want to try it another way for a change." When he scowled at me, I added, "I don't mean putting myself in danger, but maybe just taking a chance, having an adventure. I'm tired of always doing what's expected."

It was true. I had gone to college because my dad said I would. I had become a teacher because he said that, too. I married, had kids, and followed my husband as he made career moves because that was what a good little wife did.

And what had it gotten me? An unhappy marriage; an unfaithful husband, and an unexpected life change I wasn't sure I had the capacity to make. I shook off my dour musings, the bright sunshine urging me to be happy.

"While I was out yesterday, I found a place I want to rent. I need to meet with the realtor. It's a little run down, so hopefully it'll be within my price range."

Freddie raised his coffee cup to mine. "Then here's to success and adventure."

"Speaking of, what kind of adventure are you and Dennis having today?"

Freddie came to the Cape every fall, but it was Dennis' first time, so Freddie was having fun taking him here and there, showing off the best the Cape offered. "There's a winery in Truro. We'll do the tour and a little wine tasting."

"Sounds like fun."

"I want to see Martha's Vineyard, too," Dennis commented as he set his bowl of granola on the table and joined us.

"That's on my list," I said.

Freddie picked up his cell phone. "Give me your number, and we'll touch base tonight when we get back." His eyes held a glint of mischief. "Maybe I can set us up with an adventure tomorrow on Martha's Vineyard."

"Freddie," I warned. From the first, we had connected and had talked well into the night. But I really didn't know him, and wondered what I was getting into.

He held out both hands, palms up as though weighing something. "Safe or adventure? Yesterday..." He paused dramatically with one hand dropping down as though the weight of the past were too much to hold up. "Or now?" His other hand floated upward toward the bright sunshine.

I grinned. "You're right, but who's going to keep me on track once you go back to New York?"

"Oh, hon, I've got a plan for that, too." He said no more; just looked at me over his coffee cup with eyes that crinkled at the corners.

* * *

"Oh, sweetie, I can't rent you that house." The lady at HN Realty hurried from behind her desk and grabbed my hand.

She wore flowered Capri's and a tee shirt, crocs on her feet. Her blonde hair was cut short and curled about her round face. At least her hair wasn't fuzzy, I thought, sliding a hand over my head to smooth the frizz that wouldn't be confined by hair gel this morning.

"How did you ever even find that house?"

"I stopped here yesterday. Your assistant gave me the key and directions, of a sort."

"Gary? I really will have to speak to him. He's always playing...well, he just should have known better."

"Is there something structurally wrong with the house that I can't manage for a few months?"

She shook her head.

"Does it have running water and electricity?"

She made a face but nodded.

"Why not rent it to me then? It's empty." I thought I had already stated that fact when I came in.

"Well, it's..." She hesitated, looking out the window of the office, then to the pictures on the wall behind me, all of which were listed properties. She finally turned back to me. "It's for sale."

"I know that, but it's empty," I repeated, "and from the looks of it not exactly at the top of your list of showings. Why can't you rent it to me for the summer? I'm sure the owners would like to see at least a little money coming in."

She scrunched up her lips in thought.

"Look, let me rent it and if you should..." I almost said miraculously, "sell it before the end of summer, I'll move."

"It hasn't been lived in for quite awhile." She still hesitated.

"I'm not afraid of doing a little cleaning." I would later regret that statement as I actually hadn't cleaned a house in years.

"I would need a thousand dollars for three months rent. And you pay the electricity and water."

If she thought the cost would deter me, she was wrong. I nodded.

She quickly filled out a rental agreement while I waited. When it had been signed and she gave me a copy along with the extra key to the house, I handed over a check.

She snatched it out of my hands and quickly put it in a lockbox on the top of a filing cabinet. As she slammed the lid shut with a clank, she pushed the lock and extracted the key before turning to me.

"Okay, it's yours for three months but don't come back in a week and want your money back. Don't say I didn't warn you."

I walked out into the bright morning sunshine before her words sank in. Warn me about what? I turned back just in time to see her place a closed sign in the window and to hear the click of the door being locked.

* * *

It took most of the afternoon to unload my car and get stuff stored away. I had brought only my clothes, a few pictures of the kids and some of my favorite pottery, my laptop and files, and the coffeepot. Anything else I needed I could buy later. I didn't want to go back into town, but there was no help for it, considering I didn't even have a bottle of water.

I turned on the kitchen faucet, leery of drinking the water in the pipes. I let it run and did the same in the bathroom as I lugged a box of clothes up the steep steps to the loft. Damn, I didn't even have a sheet for the bed. A list was definitely in order, or I would never remember what I needed by the time I did get to town.

I knelt and peered out one of the porthole windows to where the crystal blue of the ocean beckoned me. Unpacking could wait. I grabbed my camera, kicked off my shoes on the back deck, and wandered down to the shore. The beach was a mixture of sand and rocks, and it wasn't long before I had a pocketful of various sized stones. I'd have to find a tin or dish to put them in. As I picked up yet another, I wondered how large of a pile I'd have by summer's end.

There weren't a lot of shells along the shore, but perhaps it wasn't the right time of day. I didn't know anything about the tides, but from the uneven lines of pebbles strewn along the sand, I figured it must be going out. The sun was low, but on this side of the Cape, I wouldn't see the sun set, at least not over water.

I took some pictures, standing ankle deep in water. It washed over my feet, feeling chilly yet soothing in the lingering heat of the day.

My cell rang. It was Freddie.

"Where are you?"

"I found a house to rent for the summer so I spent the day moving in. Are you and Dennis back from Truro?"

"We just got in. We did some wine tasting and then drove on to Wellfleet. What are you doing for dinner?"

"I guess I'll come back into town. I didn't take time to buy any groceries. Actually I don't even know where a grocery store is."

"Meet us at Ross' Grill about eight. It's on the second floor of Whaler's Wharf and has a great view of the harbor. We'll plan our strategy for tomorrow."

I looked at my watch. It was already seven. "I think I can make that." I started back to the cottage. I thought how regional words were. If I were in the Rocky Mountains, I would be going to a cabin, but here on the shores of Cape Cod, it was a cottage.

"Ouch." My foot turned on an unusually large rock as I stepped to shore. Beside it was a shell, drifting in the shallow water, then settling on the sand as the water left it momentarily alone.

I had no sooner taken a picture than a wave came, gently swishing the pebbles in the shell even as it pushed the shell toward shore. In a heartbeat, the water receded, taking with it some of the pebbles but depositing others in their place. I dropped to my knees, fascinated at this moment in nature that was so much larger than the actual picture I had just taken.

The pebbles of my life, I thought. My mom and dad, gone now for too many years, but in their places were my children, lighting up my life with their adventures, their laughter and their joys. As I watched, those pebbles were gone on the very next wave and they'd never return, not to this same shell on this same beach. Just like my children, I thought, gone away to new lives with new partners. Even if they returned, it would never be the same because just like the shell, no matter how hard I tried to hang on, I couldn't withstand the ever-changing tides.

Every pebble in that shell was part of me; some so microscopic as to be nothing more than bits of sand, like the baby I lost almost before I knew I was pregnant. Not one single pebble was like another, either in size, shape or color, and yet each represented part of my life—friends, family, acquaintances, events and places. Just as the pebbles washed in and out of the shell, each person had made a momentary stop to fill my heart with wonder and my soul with happiness for having known of them.

The tide was changing; larger waves swept to the shore. For a while the shell held steady in the sand, drifting slightly with the wash of water and the bubbles surrounding it, but always there once the water slid away. And always gently cradling the pebbles that had managed to remain within.

As I watched, it occurred to me all the things that shell represented: me, family, faith. The shell had once been half of a whole and home to a life before it was broken apart and now rested on the beach alone. Yet even alone, it still gathered pebbles that drifted by. Some stayed quite a while; others came and went on each wave. But always, there was room for more.

Could the ocean wash away my hurt and disappointment; the bitterness and anger of betrayal? Would I be able to find contentment with what remained within me, like the pebbles in the shell, and not grieve forever for what had washed away? Without realizing it, perhaps that was why I had come to the beach this summer. Did I dare open myself again to all that life had to offer, gathering those new people and experiences; those new emotions and cupping them gently in my heart so they stayed awhile?

How much more enjoyable it was to watch the pebbles wash about in the cup of the shell than to watch the rocks tumble onto the shore only to be washed back into the ocean, lost before anyone had the chance to see their beauty and to experience them just being here.

* * *

I dragged my body out of bed at six the next morning, took a quick shower and dressed in a cool tank and shorts. Freddie had informed me last night at dinner that we had to leave before seven in order to get to Hyannis to catch the ferry to Martha's Vineyard.

I didn't have time to make coffee but grabbed a bottle of water and a granola bar. I was in the car backing out before I realized I forgot my camera. I added a sun visor to my bag along with the camera.

I still wasn't used to the road along the wooded area before I got to Bradford Street. A jungle of bushes, trees, and foliage blocked the sun and almost obscured the path, making it feel wild and untamed and added to my sense of adventure.

I pulled into the Pilgrim's Monument parking lot, gave the man my money, and cruised slowly until I found Freddie's car. It wasn't until I parked next to him and got out that I saw an additional passenger in the back seat, and it wasn't Dennis.

Freddie had his window down.

"Freddie," I said his name in what I hoped was a threatening tone.

"Haven't you had your coffee yet?" He just smiled. "As a matter of fact..."

The back door opened and Robert motioned me in. "We can stop at a coffee shop on the way," he said as he slid across the seat.

I hadn't known he was coming. I hadn't really thought about him since the night Freddie introduced us at dinner. I didn't want to think about him. That certainly wasn't why I came to Cape Cod.

I slid into the car and shut the door, putting my beach bag between us. I gave him a weak smile, but Freddie got the brunt of my anger as I glared at him in the rear view mirror.

It took over an hour to reach Hyannis where the ferry docked, but at least we stopped for coffee on the way. I didn't understand my antagonistic attitude. Robert was a nice man, and he was friends with Freddie. I had no problem with that. After all, once Freddie left I would know at least one person in town. It didn't have to go anywhere.

Then why, I asked myself, did I keep sneaking glances his way?

Once we parked and gathered our gear, all three guys walked fast and I had to skip-step to keep up with them.

"What's the hurry?" I asked once I saw the dock on the left just half a block ahead of us.

"We want good seats," Dennis threw over his shoulder as he and Freddie surged ahead to get in the ticket line.

"That doesn't seem to be a problem," I murmured once we got on the ferry. There were more vacant seats than passengers, and I didn't see any long line still boarding. I climbed the steps to the second level, then over to where more steps led to the outside seating.

"Where did those two go?" I asked when Robert sat down beside me.

"Dennis didn't think he could handle being on deck."

"What? Riding outside and up high is like being in the very front seat of a roller coaster. It's the only way to go." I closed my eyes and tilted my head back, letting the early morning sun warm me. The ferry's horn blasted as we pulled away from the dock. The harbor was calm, and I wasn't afraid of a little wave action anyway, knowing the ferry was sturdy.

Several minutes passed in silence and I almost forgot that I wasn't alone, not on this day anyway. As the ferry made a gentle turn, Robert's leg nudged mine. He'd worn shorts today, and his legs were brown and just a little hairy. His knees were nice, too, not knobby like some guys.

When I looked his way, I found his steady gaze on me— not scrutinizing or criticizing, just observing me, maybe trying to memorize my features for when I would no longer be there.

I shook off that thought. Those things only happened in the stories I wrote. They did not happen to me in real life. Real life sucked. I broke eye contact and glanced out at the water, a beautiful crystalline blue, deeper than the sky that met it at the horizon.

"I ordered all your books last night, even the eBooks."

My gaze jerked back to his. "You what?"

He shrugged and grinned. "My bookstore could use some new authors. Maybe you would consider doing a book signing while you're here."

"You really do own a bookstore?"

"The Pokey Reader," he said. "I thought about naming it the Hokey Pokey but I didn't want people thinking I was opening a dance studio."

I laughed at his silliness. "But all my books? Why would you do that?"

"To learn about you."

"Believe me, they're all fiction."

"I know, but I've found that most authors put a little of themselves into the stories they write. It may be an incident, a favorite object, even a dream. Remember how Alfred Hitchcock would always show up in all his movies?"

I chuckled. "You're showing your age with that comment."

"Age is a state of mind. How old are you?"

"My real age or the lie I tell everyone?"

"See, that's what I mean." Rob laughed. "Anyway, I thought maybe reading your work would give me some insight as to who you are and what you want out of life."

I looked at him, trying to determine if he was serious. It had been awhile since anyone had focused on what I wanted.

He started to speak but I put up a hand. "Can we talk about something else, please?"

His brows lowered over brooding eyes and I could have kicked myself for ruining our mood. I had so very much to learn.

"I'm sorry."

He smiled a little sadly. "I'll bet you said that a lot, didn't you?"

My cheeks burned. How could he possibly know about my life and what I had gone through? How arrogant of him to even think he knew. I opened my mouth to tell him so.

"Let's make a pact," he said. "Neither of us will say anything hurtful to the other, then neither of us will have a reason to say we're sorry."

"Friends should be able to speak the truth," I countered.

"That's true, but the truth isn't hurtful; not if you're really friends."

That had been one of the problems in my marriage. My husband and I hadn't started as friends. We met in college and had jumped right into a romantic relationship. We were so young and neither had really become a true person yet. I remember being constantly worried about impressing him, or saying the wrong thing, so there had been many times I didn't say what I wanted. I couldn't tell him things a friend would tell a friend.

"Too much introspection on a sunny day is bad for you," he said.

I forced the frown from my face. "Why don't you tell me about yourself instead?"

"That may be asking for more of the same."

"Robert, I don't want to psychoanalyze you. Just give me the basics—you know—the who, what, when, where, why."

"Ah, but it's only the 'why' that you're really interested in, isn't it?"

"Why what?"

"Why I'm here; why I'm not married; why I took an interest in you?" His intense gaze held mine.

"There's just no help for us, is there?" I laughed to release the tension building inside. "We're bound and determined to ferret out each other's secrets."

"In my case, there are no secrets. The plain and simple truth is I like your laugh. I think when you allow yourself, you probably laugh a lot. It's infectious and your blue eyes light up and you get those little wrinkles at the corners." He touched the corner of my eye.

"Wrinkles? You really know how to turn a girl's head." I jabbed him with my elbow.

"Okay," he said. "Quick truths so you quit wondering. I lived in Boston most of my life. When my wife died five years ago, I moved to Provincetown and opened a bookstore. End of story."

I knew there was more to it than that, but like me, he didn't seem inclined to share. And that was fine. After all, we were only together for the day.

"So you're a 'washashore'?" I teased.

He nodded. "Yep, that's me. Just like you."

"I can't even claim that. I'm only here for the summer."

He looked out across the bay then slowly brought his gaze back to mine. "Maybe; maybe not."

* * *

The minute we got off the ferry at Oak Bluff and regrouped with Freddie and Dennis, I saw what I wanted to do.

"Let's ride the carousel." I headed up the street to the 'Flying Horses' sign. I heard distinctive male groans behind me. I turned, hands on hips, and stared at my companions.

Dennis looked hopeful. Freddie sighed with resigned indulgence and Robert looked just plain resigned.

I patiently explained. "I came here to explore and write. In order to write, I have to 'feel' the experience." When Freddie opened his mouth to say something, I kept going. "You guys dragged me out here at the crack of dawn. Now we're going to make the most of it."

"You wanted to come," Freddie protested.

"She's right, guys," Robert said, moving forward to grab my hand and pull me along. I tried to pull loose. One of the things I had missed most in the last years of my marriage

37

was physical contact. My husband had never touched me unless he wanted sex. What a paradox that I had craved hugs and simple touches, but now the contact seemed too personal.

He seemed to sense my disquiet and gently squeezed my hand. "What is the word that historical writers use when someone owes a favor? They get a 'boon'?"

"Your point is?"

"I allow you to drag me on a carousel ride, and you allow me to hold your hand." He looked down at me with a gentle smile, as though he knew how hard it was for me.

"I seriously doubt you allow anyone to drag you anywhere you really don't want to go," I said. He just grinned and tugged me along with him.

The line was impossibly long but moved quickly. As we stood waiting our turn, I thought about what he had said. Friendship, indeed any relationship, was built not only on trust but also on give and take. You give, and in return you are replenished. Unfortunately, during most of my married life, my partner had taken much more than he had ever given. And there was only so much in me to give. I wonder why I never saw that at the time and was only now realizing how long ago my issues had started. Now, what was it Robert wanted from me?

"You're trying to teach me something, aren't you?" I asked just before the gate opened for our turn on the horses.

"No." He shook his head. "I'm just trying to remind you of what you already know."

I started for one of the seats as the platform jiggled slightly beneath my feet. After all, I was an adult and the horses were for the kids. Then I realized I wanted to ride a horse, too. I didn't want to be one of the sedate, proper ladies who sat on the bench and let the world pass them by as the carousel went around.

The Flying Horses carousel was the oldest working carousel in the United States and although the horses didn't go up and down, it was fun spinning around to the tinny sounds of the pipe music. There was a small metal arm sticking out from the wall that held rings, and Robert would snag one from the holder and add it to the peg on his horse's head. The next time around he'd give one to me.

"Catching the rings dates back to the medieval jousting tournaments." He leaned over to tell me, trying to talk above the music. "The knights would try to spear a ring with their lance. It was an easy enough transition when the first carousels were invented to transfer that idea to riding inanimate horses."

"I didn't realize 'catch the brass ring' originated with carousels." The platform was slowing and the music wound down. Had carnival rides always been this short, or was it being an adult that made them seem that way?

We walked out into the bright sunshine to wait for Dennis and Freddie. They were just far enough behind us that they had to wait for the next round. "How do you know all about jousting tournaments and carousels?"

"A lot of the books in my store could be considered used, as I read constantly," Robert said, then excused himself for a minute.

I pulled out my camera to take pictures. I caught one with Robert just coming out of the building, the Flying Horses sign above his head. It was the sign I was photographing, I told myself.

He bowed before me and with a flourishing hand gesture, presented me with a brass ring, colorful ribbons hanging from it. "A brass ring for m'lady, so she always remembers to reach for the best." He winked.

I curtsied then smiled in return. "Many thanks, m'lord." With a sigh I tried to look crestfallen even though the play acting was delightful. "I suppose you will want another boon in return?"

"Of course." He grinned.

Freddie and Dennis joined us and we looked for a place to eat. The sun was hot and there was little breeze, but I insisted on eating outside when we came across the Island House, which had small tables along the sidewalk.

"I live inside, work inside, drive around inside a car—"

"We get the picture," Dennis groused as we collected around a small table.

"Besides, we can watch people this way."

We all ordered crab cake sandwiches and iced tea. The street was noisy and full of people, mostly tourists, I suspected, as their hands were full of shopping bags. As we waited for our food, the tables next to us were cleared and rearranged, and before long a large group of people took up residence: adults, kids, even two babies in strollers and one very pregnant lady.

"Is this your family?" I asked a gray haired lady who happened to sit next to me.

She beamed. "This isn't even all of them. I have eighteen grandchildren, ranging from twenty-one down to this little tyke." She bent over and tickled the baby's bare foot.

Her name was Claire, and over the course of our sandwiches and iced tea, I learned she lived in Boston but had a house on the Cape since 1954. Every year all the children and grandchildren, or as many as possible, descended and spent a week together. I envied her not only her large family, but the cohesiveness of it and all the togetherness. Doing a family vacation was never going to happen again in my life, at least not in the way family had always meant.

I tried to keep up with the conversation at my own table, but the guys had started talking sports, in which I had no interest. I didn't consider that I was on any kind of date with Robert, so I saw no reason to show attentiveness or listen raptly to a discussion of baseball stats.

Instead, somehow Claire's and my discussion circled around to writing. She told me about a writer's conference in Harwich Port every spring.

"Do you write, too?" I asked as I gave her one of my cards.

"Heavens, no. I'm a reader. I love to hear and meet many of my favorite authors." She reached out quickly to keep one of the toddlers from spilling a glass of water, laughing at his antics. "Perhaps I'll see you at the next conference. I would love to introduce a new author to my friends."

We said goodbye as her group got up to leave. I turned back to my companions in time to see Robert pick up the check for lunch. "You don't have to do that," I said.

"Just collecting boons," he said. "Never know when I'll need them."

* * *

We spent the rest of the afternoon walking the streets and peeking in shop windows. None of us were inclined to buy anything. Freddie said after sixty years of living, his house was full of knick-knacks and there were boxes in the basement that he hadn't been through in years. Robert already had a bookstore full and Dennis shared a small apartment with a friend. Still, we were tourists on this island and I felt we should support the economy, so I dragged Robert into several stores until he protested. I then settled on buying postcards to send friends back home.

Our explorations led us to a section of Oak Bluff with row upon row of gingerbread houses. Their bright multicolored exteriors were all trimmed in latticework of various patterns: lace, butterflies, and odd geometric designs. Some had belonged to families for generations, like my new acquaintance Claire. Other cottages were now rented by tourists for a week or a month in the summer. I remembered hearing people say, "I used to summer at Martha's Vineyard" and I never fully realized the meaning.

As we sat near the docks eating ice cream and waiting for the ferry to collect us, I realized what a great day it had been. Freddie and Dennis were fun to be around because Freddie, an Italian New Yorker, could talk circles around anyone so there was never a dull minute. Robert teased and joked, keeping the atmosphere light, which I sorely needed in my life right now. I loved to laugh and act silly sometimes and had done little of that in the past years.

"I enjoyed today, Robert," I said as we once again settled on the top deck of the ferry.

"Call me Rob. Robert sounds stuffy."

"And you're certainly not that."

"I used to be. Then one day I decided life was too short to go through it stuffy, or in a bad mood."

"I so totally agree. I used to tell the kids that if I knew where to buy a sense of humor, I would buy their dad two of them." I realized what I let slip, so I quickly turned my attention to the kids scooting into the row in front of us—the same ones who had been there on the trip over. I hoped Rob would just let my comment drop. It was weird that no matter how mad I was, or how I hated what my husband had done to me and our family, there were still things—events, comments, stories—that managed to just pop out when I talked.

"You're a people person, BJ," Rob said, using a nickname I wouldn't have thought of, but I liked.

"How do you know my initials?"

"I googled you." He wiggled his brows and made the word sound sexy. But my question didn't throw him off track. "Why do you want to spend the summer alone? I got the idea this morning you weren't thrilled to have me along."

"It's not you," I countered, because it really wasn't. He had been terrific today. "And you're right. I love visiting with new people and finding out new things..."

"But?"

I wasn't about to tell him my life history on a ferry in the middle of Nantucket Sound, even if chances were good I would never see him after today. Besides, I needed time to find out who I was and what I wanted, before I had anything to offer someone else. Not that he was asking for anything. Not that he wasn't a good looking man who appeared interested. I mentally groaned at my confused thoughts.

"Bonnie?"

Darn, he was persistent.

"I have...issues."

He laughed out loud, the sound rising above the noise of the engine and the wind. He wrapped an arm around my shoulders and gave me a quick hug. When I glanced his way he just smiled and winked before saying, "Is that all?"

Chapter 3
The Storm

I promised myself after the weekend with Freddie, Dennis, and Rob that I would stop being a tourist and do what I came to do: write. I set up my computer and files on the desk in the front room and tried not to be distracted by the view out the window. I didn't have any garden tools, so the sand roses continued to grow haphazardly across the front porch. Their color always perked me up as I sat drinking my morning coffee.

Get to work, I admonished as I turned back to my computer screen. After two weeks in the cottage, I was settled in nicely. Phone calls to Baltimore gained me the information and statistics I needed for a technology grant they contracted me to write. But instead of working on that, this morning I dragged out the romance novel that was my fiction work in progress, thumbing through the draft that wasn't much beyond chapter one. I quickly tossed it back into the box.

My life and emotions weren't in any shape to write romance; some days I doubted seriously if I would ever write that type of fiction again. The disappointment and hurt of betrayal still sat heavy on my shoulders. On bright, sunny days as I walked the beach or ate lunch at one of the many outdoor cafes, I could almost think I was merely on vacation and my life was as I had always known it. But at night, when I curled into bed by myself, with no one to visit with about the day and no good night kisses, I still cried.

Life was not totally bleak as I thought about Rob a lot. He gave me his number when we parted company at Pilgrim's Monument two weeks ago. When I hadn't called in two days, he did, apparently having gotten my number from Freddie.

We'd met for dinner a couple of times, but I always drove into town, meeting him at one of the many restaurants on Commercial Street. His company was nice, but I knew I had built a wall around myself. I wasn't ready to let anyone penetrate it, especially a man who might have romantic intentions. Oh, no, that would never happen to me again.

In the meantime, it was very nice visiting with a friend, and not having to tell a restaurant hostess there "would only be one" for dinner. I tipped back in my chair, recalling our conversation just last night as we sat enjoying the late evening breeze after dinner, talking about our childhoods and younger years. Rob, an only child, had lived his whole life in Boston; married right out of college and had worked as a stockbroker. I had grown up with four siblings, moved every couple of years with a military dad, and still enjoyed traveling.

"By this point in our lives, you'd think we'd be settled and happy to live out our days," Rob said. "How come there's still that need to search for something different?"

"I don't know about you, but I think it has to do with the confusing times in which we were raised. For example, I'm a product of traditional upbringing. Mom didn't work outside the home and Dad was the breadwinner. We grew up with traditional television shows like Eight Is Enough. Then one day someone started talking about women's lib. In an effort to embrace the rising tide of equal rights, I tried to maintain the traditional wife and mother roles, but also become the career woman.

"Speaking for a lot of women in my generation, we raised our children, supported and promoted our husbands into good business positions, and held down jobs of our own. I'm not saying there was anything bad about taking care of the family. It was just that in my case there was no blending of ideals between husband and wife. I was expected to do all the traditional wife and woman roles and have a job. My husband was just expected to have a job. Then all of a sudden—even though it certainly wasn't that quick—I'm middle-aged and wondering who I am and what I want from life. Did I do all I could; am I all I should be?" I laughed. "I sound like an Army recruitment commercial."

Rob laughed too. "I hear you. Speaking for the male species at that time, we had to adjust to not being king anymore. We got to share responsibility for the income, but also had to learn all those skills women were born with: child rearing, cooking..."

"Careful," I warned.

"I'd have to say my wife did a good job of helping me transition. We shared equally in all aspects of our marriage."

I was jealous, even though there was no need. "It sounds like she was a very lucky woman."

* * *

Now, as I poured myself another cup of coffee, I thought about asking Rob out to the cottage for dinner. I looked around the small space. It wasn't that I didn't want him to see how I lived; the place was nice enough. Maybe I just wasn't ready to share my sacred space.

I decided to take a break from my grant writing and drive to Race Point and Herring Cove to take pictures. I hoped something in the area would give me a story idea, because I'd promised my editor a new outline by the end of the month. I wasn't a photojournalist, but sometimes I submitted pictures with the articles I wrote for magazines. It was additional money if the editor liked them and had room in the issue.

There weren't a lot of people in the water at Herring Cove. I walked barefoot, my feet sinking in the soft, wet sand. The water felt cool on my legs as waves splashed onto shore. I found an interesting rock that looked like a shrunken tomato or potato—all kind of grooved and orangish—and tucked it into my pocket to add to my collection.

Two older men sat in beach chairs, their fishing poles high in the air. I could barely see the fishing line that arched out into the water.

"With the waves washing into shore, how do you keep your bait and line out in the surf?" I asked one of them.

"It's weighted," he replied. He was darkly tanned, his face wrinkled, reminding me somewhat of the rock I had just found.

"What's biting?"

"Not much. There should be some stripers. Mostly I'm just out here to see who stops and asks questions."

I laughed. "And I bit, didn't I?"

He just grinned, and then pointed to a fast moving boat. "Did you just see that whale? Look, there goes the whale watching boat." He laughed. "By the time it gets to the site, those whales will be somewhere else entirely."

I squinted toward the horizon, staring hard at the water close to the boat. I didn't see anything.

"Don't try so hard," the old man said. "Just let your gaze sweep the area. The harder you look, the less you see sometimes."

I did as he instructed, and like magic, there was a plum, followed by a dark shape curving up and then back down into the water. It was too far away to be distinctive, but he was right; the whales were there. As I waved goodbye and continued down the beach, I wondered if his advice about not trying so hard could be applied to other life lessons.

As I picked up a rock here and there the sun baked down on my back. I squinted into the distance to Race Point lighthouse, my destination, and I was glad I had brought a bottle of water. Maybe I should have tried to find the road to the point, instead of walking the beach. But then I would have missed the fun of walking, keeping an eye on the ever-changing shoreline as the tide came in. I kept hoping I'd find a gold sovereign or something, washed ashore after hundreds of years at the bottom of the sea in some shipwrecked vessel.

"Well, it could happen," I muttered, eyeballing the lighthouse again and deciding I needed to start taking shortcuts instead of following the curve of beach. It was still a good distance, and I was getting really hot. I waded through a tide pool but when I reached the edge of a grassy area that surrounded the lighthouse I discovered it was roped off because it was the nesting ground for wild birds. I followed the stakes and strings until I stood close enough for a good picture.

Race Point lighthouse was one of only a few that had light keepers staying on site. Race Point even had rooms to rent in the Keeper cottage and I had thought about reserving one, but now was glad I hadn't. As sure as I was that a road led into the place, I probably couldn't have found it. I had had a hard enough time finding my cottage the first time.

I focused the camera, making sure I had the keeper house and the wind turbine in the shot. It wasn't surprising they took advantage of wind power as there always seemed to be a breeze offshore. When I pushed the button, there was no shutter release; no sound at all from the camera. I checked to make sure I had it on. While I loved taking pictures with this camera because it had a wide angle lens with a great telephoto, I always had it on automatic because I didn't know anything about stop speeds and...whatever. I just liked to point and shoot. And if something didn't work, I was screwed.

I turned the camera off and back on, refocused but it still didn't work. "I did not struggle through the sand clear down here in the hot sun and then not be able to take a picture," I muttered.

I sighed, thinking I really needed to take a photography class. I pushed the tiny buttons switching from people to landscapes to distance, trying again to take a picture. Still nothing. I pushed the timer, then the shutter button and finally heard the shutter swish.

Aha! If I could use the timer, at least my walk wouldn't be wasted. I turned and focused just on the lighthouse, pushed the timer then the shutter button, and held my breath to keep the camera steady...steady...steady. I just about gave up when it clicked.

I had no idea if these pictures would turn out or be fuzzy because I couldn't hold the camera steady, but I took another of the lighthouse, keeper house and wind turbine, once again utilizing the timer. As I walked back the way I had come, I tried to remember if I had seen a camera shop anywhere on Commercial Street. It would be worth having an expert take a look, as I had the whole summer ahead of me and didn't want to be without a camera.

The guys who had been fishing were gone now, but a large family had practically set up residence on the beach.

They had two free-standing canopies, lots of lawn chairs and blankets and a small bonfire going in the middle of it all. I watched, envious of their laughter, as a young adult talked to an elderly lady—probably the grandmother of them all—and a dad picked up his baby daughter, swinging her high in the air amid gurgling laughter.

I lifted my camera and took a shot, not realizing until I had done so that it worked perfectly fine without having to use the timer. What the heck was the deal with that?

* * *

It wasn't until midway through the third week that I finally bought a pair of clippers to prune the wild sand roses, so a path actually became visible from the front of the house around one side to the deck. I hadn't touched anything along the front as I liked the wild look when I drove up the path. Besides, I never used the front door.

It felt good to be active; to do something for me and to see actual results, although I had to admit I wasn't used to this kind of hard work, and I was hot and sweaty. I carefully gathered the last of the prickly branches and headed to the brush pile I had started. I looked up as a bird called overhead and that's when I noticed the cupola. It straddled the peak of the roof but wasn't in the middle lengthwise. In fact, it sat almost to the very end of the cottage. I looked down then back up. It appeared to be directly over the kitchen or dining room area.

I lifted my tee shirt to wipe my face. I'd had enough yard work for today and besides, I needed to get some real work done—the kind that paid the bills. I grabbed a bottle of water from the fridge, which rattled and grumbled every time I opened the door, then walked through the archway into the living room, looking up. There was no trap door in the ceiling that might open to the cupola.

Oh, for Pete's sake. The bedroom was upstairs. Any trap door on the living room ceiling would only open to the floor of the loft. I walked down the hall toward the painting on the door that led to the loft.

The first time I had seen it in daylight, I had let out a loud shriek, thinking someone was in the cottage. I hadn't decided if the painting was a pirate, but it was some kind of musketeer-era man, with a huge hat and flowing cape. Black breeches were tucked into tall boots. The painting took up the entire door which made the man larger than life. That first time, once my heartrate returned to normal, I had cautiously approached, because the man's eyes, dark and sinister, made it feel as if he was watching me. His right hand held a cane, the knob of which was actually the doorknob, and that made it rather spooky every time I opened the door. Even after weeks at the cottage, the vivid painting still gave me the creeps.

I hurriedly climbed the stairs, shaking off thoughts of marauding pirates. At least my imagination was starting to kick into gear. The sun was directly overhead, dusty rays of light filtering across the bedroom. The roof top solar windows were great in providing light, but they also heated up the bedroom and I hated to keep the window AC going. How hard could it be to put in some kind of slide blind? I looked around for something to measure the window and stopped.

I was doing it again, jumping from one activity to another without finishing what I started. I could walk into a room, or open a drawer, then not remember what I needed. Sometimes, I even went back to where I started until something there triggered a thought about what I had wanted in the first place.

I'm sure my counselor would say it was the physical manifestation of my current state of mind. I was trying to sort out my life and the pieces seemed scattered in a million different directions or hidden away in a dozen secret compartments. I didn't know what I wanted, nor did I have any kind of idea in what direction I was headed. I had invested so many years in my marriage that I didn't know who I was as an independent person. All that mental confusion had me scurrying from activity to activity with no sense of reason.

At the moment, I knew I hadn't come upstairs to measure the windows for blinds. I deliberately turned to the other end of the loft, carefully inspecting the ceiling for a trap door that would lead to the cupola. None existed. Why would someone put a structure on top of the cottage that had no access and no purpose other than decorative?

I scoffed. What was the big deal? Lots of places had things that served no purpose.

I grabbed some clean clothes and went downstairs to shower, hoping to put the mystery from my mind. One of the problems I hoped to solve this summer was my tendency to dwell on things until I stressed out about them. And the really stupid part was, they were usually things that I couldn't do a damn thing about.

I couldn't fix my ex's behavior or what he had done that tore our family apart. I had cajoled and cried and begged and pleaded and he hadn't changed. I didn't know if he was even capable of change, but I couldn't do it for him. And now, I couldn't do anything about the basic structure of the cottage, not that the two things were even remotely related. I cranked on the shower and climbed in.

Let it go.

* * *

Some days are so productive. I sighed, pushing back from the old roll-top desk. I had completed the rough draft for a major technology grant for one of my main clients and then composed two articles for a couple of magazines to which I regularly submitted. All my work was rough, and I'd let it simmer for a day before revising. I was very lucky I had the capability to work freelance. I hadn't had to quit a job when I left home. A laptop and internet connection in today's market were invaluable. Once in a while I had to go directly to a client for data and personal information from associates but since I loved to travel, a day trip to Boston or Philly was never out of line. The fact the contracting agent paid for it was a bonus.

Wandering into the kitchen for a glass of wine, I took it out onto the deck to unwind. The wind hit me the instant I opened the door. Late afternoon, even facing east, brought color to the sky, but today a yellowish cast blended with the usual pinks and oranges of sunset.

I scooted the lounge away from where it had been blown against the side of the house. I wondered if a storm was brewing. I supposed I should get a radio on one of my trips to the store.

I had no sooner settled than I heard my cell ring. I didn't get many calls, so I rarely carried it on my person. I sighed. Did I even want to answer it?

Rob—his name floated across my mind. I swung a leg over the side of the chaise and paused. He'd already called twice today, wanting to come out. I told him I was working. The second time he called to invite me to dinner. He didn't seem to understand I was here to work.

I grinned. It was sort of nice being pursued, even if I wasn't in the market for any kind of relationship. Rob was nice to be around, and he made me laugh.

Both feet slammed to the deck, and I made a dash for the door only to be met with silence. Damn, I missed his call— well, if it had been him. I looked at the read-out and smiled. I seemed to be doing that a little more lately.

I punched redial. "Hey," I said when he answered.

"Are you okay?"

"Yeah, why?"

"There's a storm coming, and it's supposed to be bad. I'm closing the store early. Why don't you come in and stay at my house?"

My heart pounded. What would we do at his house? I reminded myself we were just friends and that was how I liked it.

"I'll be fine, Rob. I can't run into town for every little thing."

"This isn't every little...what was that?" he asked at the same time I heard a distinctive groan, followed by a flash of lightning and then thunder.

My heart thudded now for an entirely different reason. "Thunder," I replied, hurrying over to light a candle then another, in case the lights went out. There should be another hour of daylight, but the kitchen had gotten suddenly dark.

"Hello, BJ, you still there?"

"Yeah. I'm just trying to light some candles."

"Lights out?"

"Not yet." Thunder rumbled so close it shook the house. The rain started pounding the roof. "Gotta go." I tucked the phone in my pocket and quickly raced around the house shutting windows. I reached for the ledge over the bathtub when more moaning erupted, followed by deep throated swearing.

I screamed.

I rushed into the living room making sure the door was locked. The house creaked and moaned. I swore the floor in the kitchen rolled beneath my feet as I reached the back door.

The house...moaned. I felt a little better thinking it was the wind and storm battering the house that caused the noise and not some pervert outside my window.

My phone rang, practically giving me a heart attack.

"Talk to me." Rob's deep voice and those few words calmed me.

"It's raining."

"I need more than that to tell you're okay."

"You sound grumpy. Did you get wet going home?"

"It's not even raining here yet, but the sky looks like sh...bad out your way."

As we talked I put on a pot of coffee. The house still creaked and moaned in the wind.

"I could come out." His voice sounded, not pleading exactly, but hopeful.

More moaning and groaning, sounding like it came from the roof now.

"What is that noise? I heard it before."

"It's just the house and the wind." I looked toward the ceiling. Maybe if I kept telling myself that, I would believe it.

He sighed. "It's the kind of night when it's nice to curl up on a couch and just listen to it rain."

"Well then, do that." I knew what he was implying but liked to tease him.

"I don't mean alone. Damn, you make it hard to be romantic, even from a distance."

He was right. I could write romance—I used to write romance—but for the past several years it had all been my imagination. I hadn't lived a romantic life at all. "I'm sorry, you're right. I made coffee and was going to curl up on the couch and think of you. Does that help?"

This time I heard a sigh of frustration.

"Good night, Rob," I said with a smile. "Thanks for calling to check on me."

* * *

I groaned, rolling off the couch and coming to my feet. I had taken a cup of coffee and a book to the living room after I talked to Rob but didn't remember falling asleep. I headed to the kitchen with my cold coffee.

"Oh, God, not again."

It was the...sound. I couldn't describe it, wasn't sure where it came from, and more to the point, wasn't sure I wanted to know. The low moan continued and unless I listened carefully, it sounded just like distant thunder. But it wasn't. It sounded gurgling, underwater, and ended with muttering, too low to understand.

I jumped at a screech, followed by more moaning. I spun wildly. Lightning flashed and the lights flickered once before going out. The wind whipped branches against the side of the house and window, the heavy thumping and spine-shivering screech shooting my heart rate to a dangerous level. I swore the first thing tomorrow I would cut that tree down, if I had to hack it with a kitchen knife.

Another howl had me turning in circles. That hadn't come from the window, or the storm. Whatever it was, the creature was on the roof. I automatically looked up, then cursed because it was black as pitch. Fumbling my way along the counter, I found and lit two lanterns. The earlier lit candles, now sitting on the end table in the other room, were way too far away for me to find in the dark.

Weak yellow-gold light spread in a small circle, then turned rose-red. I had thought the old lamps so romantic when I found them in the shed and cleaned them up, but—

Thump! Thump! I dropped to a crouch by the cupboard.

That was a new noise. What the hell was on my roof? Continuous lightning gave me enough light to get into the living room where I lit the larger candle. I felt better even though the flickering light cast weird shadows on the wall as I crept down the hall. The rain was harder now, whipping against the house with the wind. I lifted the candle higher as I approached the end of the hall and screamed.

"Damn it all!" I placed my hand over my heart. "I swear you are going in the attic," I shouted at the full sized portrait that blocked my path to the loft. As many times as I went upstairs, heaving the heavy door open where the painting hung, it still scared the begezzus out of me at night.

My heart pounded. Had his eyes moved? I tried to hold the light steady on his face—the face of a tyrant; mean, cynical, cruel even. It was a trick of the light or remembered horror movies from my youth. There had always been a portrait with moving eyes, the villain hiding behind the wall to spy on unsuspecting victims.

Thump! Thump! Yo! The noise and whatever devil created it definitely came from upstairs...or from behind this painting.

I scooted back down the hall. I needed help. I needed...I grabbed my cell and hoped it still worked in the storm.

Rob answered on the first ring. "I was ready to call you, but last time—"

"Help," I whispered, crouching again in the corner.

"Someone, something's upstairs!"

* * *

Rob came barreling into the cottage, water pouring off his yellow slicker onto the rug at the door. I launched myself at him, wrapping my arms around his waist.

"Why didn't you head to town? Don't you have a radio on?" His arms came around me in a reassuring hug. He sounded angry, but I didn't care. I just stood in the circle of his wet, rubbery embrace and tried to pull myself together.

"BJ?"

"What? No, I don't have a radio, like it would do me any good since there's no electricity either." I stepped away from him, looking down at my totally soaked tee shirt. When I glanced up, his gaze was intense, the soft red and gold glow from the lanterns highlighting his high cheekbones and the tight set of his lips. "Are you mad?"

"Gee, there's driving rain and winds at forty miles per hour, and you never even gave me the directions to get out here." He tore off his slicker, tossing it toward the hook by the door. "Why would I be mad?" His floppy hat followed, missing the hook and landing on the floor with a plop.

"If it's so bad, why did you come at all?"

"Because you called in a panic. Because you're out here at the end of the earth and too stubborn to come in."

My heart warmed at the idea he cared. It had been a long time since another person had put me before himself. I had to admit it felt good and it made me want to give back. I took a step toward him and stopped. Now that the trauma had passed, I felt shy about having grabbed him the way I had. As much as I thought I wanted touching, and hugs, closeness and affection, I couldn't bring myself to initiate it. How pathetic was that?

"I looked around outside with a flashlight before I came in but didn't see anything. What's going on, anyway?"

I tilted my head to the side. Even though the wind still blew, and rain still drummed on the roof, I didn't hear the sound anymore. Maybe it was just Rob's presence, but it didn't feel as frightening.

"Just noise, I guess. I must have panicked, this being the first storm and all."

Rob rubbed a hand over his face, peeking at me one eye at a time as his hand slid down. "Is that coffee still hot?"

I touched the glass. "Warm." I filled a couple of mugs while Rob collected the French Vanilla creamer and a spoon. He hadn't used cream in his coffee before he met me.

Thunder still rumbled outside, and it didn't sound like the storm was lessening. I cocked an ear. Maybe the sounds I had heard were just part of the storm. Maybe it hadn't been groans and whispers and words just beyond understanding.

"What's really going on?" Rob placed his warm hand over mine on the counter. The surprising touch, more intimate than the casual ones we'd shared, sparked something deep inside that scared me. I snatched my hand back. To cover my feelings of awkwardness, I took a sip of coffee.

He waited, his gentle gaze flickering from mine to the lanterns then back. If there was one thing I had learned about Rob over the past weeks, he had the patience of Job and the tenacity of a bulldog. He wasn't going to forget this, and his question didn't really have anything to do with the storm.

"There's so much you don't know about me—so much that I don't really know about myself. And it's hard to know where to start."

He shrugged. "Any place will do."

"I used to work for public television. There was a pledge spot we ran about a water cooler. You know, like the kind they have in offices." At his nod, I continued, not sure if my story would even make sense in what I was trying to tell him about myself. "Anyway, the water cooler started out full, but they kept putting crocks under it with program names on them, taking away full crocks of water. The water represented money for programming. Finally, they put a crock under the spigot for new programming but there was no more water in the cooler."

"And this is like a fable about your life?" he asked gently. "That everybody took and took and never gave back so now you have nothing to give?"

"Well, not everybody, but...yes."

"Can I see?"

"See what?" I was confused.

"The spigot in your belly button." He grinned.

My mouth dropped open. "You are such a...did you even listen?"

He laughed outright then. "I did, and the first thing I'm going to dump back into your water cooler is a sense of humor."

"Oh, God, I used to say that about my ex-husband. I can't be that bad."

He pulled my resisting body next to his, even though my shirt was still wet. "No, not at all. Maybe instead I'll put in a bunch of memory. Sometimes, when things get really bad, we tend to forget the good times, the humor, and the love." He grabbed my hand in his, reached for one of the lanterns and I caught the other as he tugged me into the living room. We carefully put the lanterns on the table in front of the couch. I needed to remember to buy more small candles if I was going to have summer storms like this very often.

When Rob sat down on the couch, I curled up on the opposite end, my feet cross legged under me and turned toward him, but with a good distance between us. He looked from the empty space to me, then casually crossed his feet on the coffee table and tucked his hands behind his head.

"Do you really think someone was out in the storm, trying to break into this place?" He looked around.

"It's not that bad." I took offense on behalf of my little cottage.

"I don't mean the cottage itself, but just trying to break in; maybe get out of the storm, not realizing anyone was living here now."

I shivered. "I prefer to think it was the wind, oh, and one damned tree that's going to be cut down tomorrow."

Rob's presence was a quiet one, yet his gentle strength made me feel safe, and oddly comfortable.

"We could watch TV," he commented idly.

"There's no electricity," I replied, then laughed. "There's no TV either."

"What about a movie on your computer?" His gaze slid to the desk.

"I do have a couple, but I'm not sure the battery is full power. What if we got almost to the end and the battery died? We wouldn't know what happened."

He thought about that for a minute. "So, we sit?"

I squirmed and fidgeted.

"I started reading one of your books." He broke the silence. "You are a very gifted writer. The plots are unique, and the relationships are awesome, if a little too perfect."

"Romance readers want happily ever after. Who wants to read the sad circumstances of one's own life? It's like the movies for me. If I pay to see a movie, I want to enjoy it. I don't want to leave feeling sad, or dissatisfied, or unsettled. Books should end happy because life doesn't always."

"It can."

"How can you say that? Your wife died." I could have bitten my tongue.

"But my life isn't over yet."

I decided to change the subject. "You know, I don't even know your last name."

"Garrett. I was going to name my bookstore The Garrett but it's on the ground floor instead of a loft. I decided on The Pokey Reader."

"Because Hokey Pokey was taken," I finished, remembering his story when we first met.

"Yeah." His gaze captured mine. Even in the minimal light from the lanterns, I could tell he was intense, wondering, hoping. I had sometimes written that a character's eyes were the mirror to his or her soul, but had never really felt it, until now. Could he see into my head in a similar way? Would he turn tail and run if he saw the confusion, the doubt, the unhappiness?

"Now that we've been formally introduced, come here." He wiggled his index finger.

I stayed at my end of the couch. "Why are you trying to fix me?"

He smiled. "You're not broken, BJ. I think you're just a little...cracked, that's all."

I laughed. "That makes me feel better."

"You know what I mean." Before I could scoot, he bent forward, taking me by the arms and dragging me down to his end of the couch. I stiffened, trying to pull away but his arm was snug around my waist, holding me still.

"It's okay. Just be still, I'm not going to do anything."

Silent tears coursed down my cheeks. The weight of his arm felt good. Sitting with my back propped against his chest felt good, so what was I afraid of? Wasn't this what I wanted in a relationship—the touching, the tactile sensations I had been missing all these years?

I felt his lips in my hair, lightly kissing my head, trailing down toward my ear. Ha! I should have known it wouldn't end with a touch.

I pushed against him, and he released me, letting me sit up, but his hand still caressed the back of my neck. I couldn't look at him, but instead stared into the darkness.

"Did he hurt you?" I could hear anguish in his voice on my behalf.

"Not in the way you think. He didn't hit me. In fact, just the opposite. He never touched me unless..." I didn't know how to tell him except to just blurt it out. "It got to the point where we never touched, because for him, the slightest touch on my part was an invitation. Touching meant sex. My husband couldn't hug me or sit next to me without it leading to sex—rather bad sex actually. I so missed the tactile closeness."

"So, you don't want touching or sex?"

"Yes...no. It's so confusing." I sighed. "I felt sometimes like the experiment with the monkeys where they gave one an inanimate surrogate mother, but the other monkey had nothing to touch or be touched by. And the one without any touching died. That's how I felt—like some part of me died. I didn't miss the sex, but I missed the touching. I know I need to get past it but now I can't seem to separate the two."

His hand had paused while I spoke, but now it moved again, lightly caressing, his thumb circling my ear. "So, it's just sex you don't want?"

I shrugged, though my body was throbbing in places I hadn't felt in a very long time.

"It's too much work. I had to..." I couldn't say what I was thinking. "It just wasn't worth it in the end."

"You never want it?" The way he said the word, like he was being forced into a monastery where he'd never see a woman again, almost made me smile.

But I was still shaking my head.

"That's a really, really long time."

I could tell by his tone he didn't agree with me, yet he still sat there; still touched me. He didn't jump up and run out the door because he wasn't going to get any. I had told myself from day one that all men weren't like my ex. Other people—women as well as men—had told me that too. And on an intellectual level I believed it. But on an emotional plane, where I still hurt so much at the way he treated me, on that level I was still too fragile; still broken at least in spirit regardless of what Rob had said.

But when I looked into soft gray eyes and saw a smile that was tender and just for me, I thought that maybe here was the man with the super glue to fix me.

"Maybe not never," I whispered. "Just not right now."

He pulled me back against him. I closed my eyes and let contentment swirl around the edges of me, not quite ready to let it completely inside. I felt Rob's chest rise and fall on a sigh.

"Well, that's a relief."

Chapter 4
Floating Houses

I woke the next morning on the couch, covered with a light throw. The storm had passed, and the sun was out. I sat up, stretching, arching to get the kink out of my back. It was not the most comfortable place to sleep. As I stood, I smelled coffee.

"Rob?" I wandered around the end of the couch and into the kitchen. "I didn't mean to fall asleep..." I was talking to myself. The kitchen was empty, although the coffee pot gurgling on the counter meant he hadn't left that long ago. I went and looked out the front window, but his jeep was gone.

Now why was I disappointed? I didn't want a relationship...I didn't need a man in my life...I didn't...

"Augh! I don't know what I want." I grabbed a coffee mug from the cupboard and poured in the creamer. It wasn't until I reached for the pot that I saw Rob's note, scribbled on the bottom of my 'To Do' list.

Actually, leaving you was as chivalrous as I could get. We both would have been in trouble if I carried you to your bedroom. To tell the truth I'm not sure where you do sleep in this tiny cottage, but I intend to find out.

My hand shook as I poured coffee. I wasn't afraid of Rob. The fact that he was warning me of things to come wasn't even a threat. It was a spine tingling, thrilling prophecy. It was like being young again and in the first bloom of sexual awareness with the pursuit, the give and take, the slow awakening of passion. Yet because of our ages, we had experiences already, and if I was careful, I could learn from my past mistakes and not repeat them.

I sat down at the table with my coffee and a granola bar and started a list of what I wanted. The first couple of things were easy. I wanted trust, laughter, and friendship. I needed understanding, support, hugs. Then I realized I had started at the wrong place. Before I could make demands on another person for what I needed in a relationship, what did I have to offer; who was I?

That page proved difficult. I had to take a good look at who I was; not just to know what I had to offer another person, but if there were things about me I didn't like, I would have to make some changes. I started out easy, because I knew when I got to the nitty-gritty, I wasn't necessarily going to like what I saw. I was a middle-aged woman, a mother, a sister—oh man, I was already in trouble if part of what I brought to a relationship were my weird sisters. Well, they weren't all weird, and my brother was okay. Realizing I was getting off track, I flipped to a new page.

I am...a writer. When I had first confronted my husband about his infidelity, he had told me he had problems with my romance writing, wondering where I was doing my research, or rather with whom. When I thought back, that wasn't the first time he'd accused me of having an affair and I realized his accusations were apparently him juxtaposing his own guilt onto me.

It would do me little good now to wonder how many times he'd been unfaithful. How naïve I had been all those years ago, believing everything he told me. "Trust me," he would say, as he left for a motorcycle rally where naked women danced on the stages and ran around collecting strings of beads. How do I trust, I would wonder when I went through his things and found packages of beads and disposable cameras. Because he had destroyed my trust, it was very hard now to put my faith in someone else.

He also didn't want me sharing my books with the wives of any of his associates. Instead of being proud of my published efforts, he felt it was a bad reflection on him that his wife wrote "sleazy romance." The truth was, he never read the majority of what I wrote. I was so astonished at what he said, so hurt, that I didn't tell him several of his associates' wives bought every romance I published. The reason? Both they and their spouses read them and were overjoyed at the improvement in their love lives.

For eight months from that point until the time I moved out of the house, I couldn't write another word. Not just romance, but there was no Christmas story card that year, a tradition I had created and carried on for over ten years. He had taken away my desire and my creativity because he used my romance writing as an excuse for his own adultery. Words that once held such joy in expressing my characters' relationships and love now seemed sordid and nasty. He made me ashamed and embarrassed by what I wrote, even though everything I wrote was not romance.

If I were to have a relationship with another person, he would have to accept my writing in all its varying venues—fiction as well as nonfiction. If I said "I am a grant writer" that had to be okay, but if I said "I am a romance writer" that had to be okay, too.

I am…a giving person. I smiled as I remembered what Rob had said about the spigot. I would do anything for our children and my family and friends. I would have given away my last dime if someone needed it, but at the end of my marriage I hadn't been giving, at least not toward my husband. I felt that trait was still part of who I was, but realized that in order for me to give, it was just as important for me to receive. So if I am a giving person, I needed to find—I flipped back to page one and added this important factor to my needed list—another giving person.

I realized as I was writing that the two sections I was trying to keep separate were really two halves of a whole, like the shells I had found on the beach. I couldn't identify who I was and what I had to give without tying it to what I wanted. Being a writer, no matter what genre, needed acceptance giving needed replenishing. Everything I wrote—trust, happiness, laughter—were things I had to give, not just be on the receiving end.

That was the—well, maybe not the breaking point, but close—of my marriage. I had become tired of constantly giving and not receiving—respect, trust, help, commitment—everything that is so important to any relationship even if it's only friendship. I just couldn't keep giving it all away and not get anything in return; no matter how good of a person I tried to be.

A lot of what I wanted to give in a relationship I had to find in myself again first. My trust was shattered, my respect for myself as a woman and writer was tarnished. The happiness and laughter were perhaps a little easier to find because I still took pleasure in the simple things—a walk on the beach, a child's laughter, having someone make me coffee in the morning.

I smiled and picked up the notepad with Rob's dark, scribbled a note. I wondered idly how long he had stayed last night after I went to sleep, apparently on his shoulder. I glanced down at my notes. Rob had so many qualities I said I wanted. Was I projecting what I thought I saw in him onto my desires? I didn't think so.

He hadn't scoffed at my reticence to cuddle; hadn't told me I was being silly when I called, scared in the storm. He was a good person—probably better than I deserved.

I slammed down my coffee cup, lecturing myself. I am a good person and I deserve good things. I am not guilty, and I have no reason to be ashamed. I am only guilty of trying to hang on to my marriage long after I should have let go. How long would it take for that message, which I repeated daily, to become part of me? I stood, knowing that stewing about it wouldn't help. If I wanted to be positive, I needed to be around positive people.

I grinned. *If that's the excuse you want to use to see Rob, it works for me.*

* * *

I gathered my dirty clothes and went into town to do laundry. I mailed my latest grant proposal to Baltimore and picked up some groceries. The day promised to be just as hot as the one previously. My tank top and shorts were going to be worn out by summer's end, and the Capri's and sweaters I had brought were still packed away in a suitcase.

I stopped at the bookstore last. It was the first time I had actively sought Rob out, other than calling him in the storm, and he acted delighted to see me. It was only the middle of the day, but when I mentioned that I bought steaks, he locked up the store and we headed back to my place.

"Good God, BJ, you should call this the end of the world instead of the end of the lane," he commented as the car bounced over the uneven lane.

"You've been out here before," I countered.

"Only in the dark." He instinctively ducked as I drove under a low hanging branch. Used to it by now, I didn't even flinch.

"I prefer to think of it as the beginning," I said, referring to his 'end of the world' comment.

"You never did tell me about that." Robert followed me into the house where I threw my keys on a side table. I knew to what he referred, but wasn't ready to talk about it. "We've only known each other a few weeks. Why would you want my life history?"

I opened the fridge and deposited my groceries. When I turned back around, he took a step toward me and very cautiously lifted a hand to tuck my hair behind my ear. I shivered at the unexpected pleasure his touch caused.

"I want to know everything about you—what childhood diseases you had, whether you made good grades in school, when you lost your virginity, why you're spending the summer in Cape Cod away from any family and friends."

Of course, I knew it was coming. I might not have dated for an eternity, but there was always a time when secrets were ousted, if a relationship was to make progress.

The problem? I was still getting used to someone who cared about me and was interested in what I thought or did. It had been a long time since that had happened. Then there was the very nice feeling I anticipated when he touched me like he was doing now. It wasn't sexual; it was far more intimate, and I wasn't used to that at all. He was trying to understand me and seemed intent on gently wooing me. The problem was, the physical element was just a small part of me that had to heal. Even though I had just gone over all this in my head that very morning, I wasn't crazy about implementing it.

I stepped away from him, but when I turned, he simply pulled my back against his chest. Maybe it was better this way, where I didn't have to face him and see his thoughts written on his face.

"The hurt is still very deep, and it's difficult to talk about." Could I ever easily discuss the betrayal of trust, the lies and accusations, or the feelings of unworthiness?

"The hurt will pass," he whispered next to my ear. "Believe me, I know."

Now I felt really bad, remembering his wife had died. Here I wanted to wallow in self-pity, when there were good men like Robert who had been dealt worse blows. "Do you want to talk about it?"

He released me. "Some day," he said, "but not now. In fact, let's forget I asked for the time being. I want to take a closer look at this place you were gullible enough...uh, lucky enough to rent."

"I still don't know what the problem is. Everybody seems to know exactly where this house is, and everyone thinks I'm crazy to have rented it, but no one will tell me why."

"It's haunted." The flat statement drifted across the living room as Rob wandered, looking at the paintings on the wall and peeking out the window.

"Oh, well, if that's all," I replied with a touch of humor, but inside my stomach knotted, recalling the strange and terrible sounds during last night's storm.

"I'm serious. In the five years I've lived in P'town, I've heard three times that many stories about a haunted cottage and probably five times as many people have come and gone from the place. Until last night, I just never connected the place everyone talked about with this particular cottage."

"So, what happens? Do I need to worry about ghosts coming after me with knives or hatchets?" I don't think he meant to scare me, but he certainly was.

"The stories I've heard are never specific. Everyone just assumes you'll understand if they say haunted. If it truly is, I imagine when it happens, you'll know." He shook his head and wandered down the hall to stand, legs braced, and hands clasped behind him, studying the portrait that was too heavy for me to remove from the door.

"Who is this, I wonder?" he said, looking over his shoulder at me, giving me that crooked smile of his. Now I knew he was simply teasing. If there were really something to the house being haunted, he wouldn't be so cavalier.

"Oh, no," I shook my head. "If you won't answer my question, I'm not answering yours."

"Ha! You don't know." He walked back past me and grabbed my hand, pulling me along in his wake. "Let's go."

"Rob." I tugged but not very hard. His grip was firm and warm, and I liked holding hands with him. "I can't play tourist all the time. I came here to write."

"You said you just put your business work in the mail, so now you get some time off."

"What about the steaks I bought? What about checking out this place?"

"We'll be back in time for sunset."

I had come to realize that no one in the area, tourists or residents, ventured out to eat until nightfall. Part of it was probably the heat, but Commercial Street didn't come alive until well past nine at night.

By this time, he had managed to get me outside the house, and he shut the door behind me.

"I didn't lock it or grab my purse."

"BJ, do you honestly think anyone can find this place, much less want to break into it?" He glanced around the exterior.

"It's not that bad, you know."

"Besides, the construction on this house looks familiar, so I'm taking you on a research field trip. Then you can't say you're not working."

I gave up. I could blame him for disrupting my day, but in truth, I had sought him out because I liked his company. He talked to me, listened to my ideas, and laughed. His sense of humor probably endeared him to me more than anything else, and it certainly made points on that list of needs I had started earlier.

He grabbed my keys and now slid into the driver's seat.

"Hey." I stood in front of the car, hands on hips.

"You drive crazy. Get in." He reached over and pushed open the passenger door.

"Maybe I just drive you crazy." I stuck my tongue out at him as I buckled my seatbelt.

"Yeah; maybe." He winked as he backed the car around in a tight circle, then stomped on the gas to bounce us along the sand road before swerving onto the blacktop.

"You were kidding, right, about me driving crazy? I mean if this is the standard by which you judge crazy..." My comment trailed off as he reached over and tugged me toward him with a hand to the back of my neck. Before I could register his intent, he kissed me, let me loose and put his hand back on the steering wheel.

"Damn," he swore as he swerved slightly to the right, letting up on the gas.

A horn honked as a car sped by in the opposite direction. I blinked, still leaning toward him. He was staring straight ahead, intent on the narrow roadway as several more cars passed.

It occurred to me that I needed to say something. "We could have been killed."

He gave me a grin; that slightly crooked, clear to the twinkling eyes grin that was rapidly melting my defenses against getting involved. "Naw," he said, "I looked first."

* * *

"It occurred to me," Rob said minutes later after he parked and opened my car door for me, "after seeing your place in the light of day instead of the middle of a thunderstorm, that there may be some historic significance to it. It's very similar in design to this." He pointed to a smallish house squeezed in-between two larger buildings near the east end of Commercial Street. "It's the Joseph Conrad Gallery and is purported to be one of the oldest structures in Provincetown."

He led me through the door of the gallery, which contained paintings of Cape Cod seascapes, lighthouses, and other local sites. Some were watercolors, others, pastels or oils.

"Do you think there's a picture of the cottage?"

"No, no," Rob replied. "It's not the art we're here to see—"

"Well, get your arse out of my place then," a voice grumbled before the body it belonged to came out from behind a dividing wall. "Joe Conrad," he said, stretching his hand to me. "You really need to stay away from riffraff like him." He nodded toward Rob.

"Hi. Bonnie Keeler." I returned his handshake. Joe was a tall, nice looking man wearing a paint splattered Looney-Tunes shirt.

The two men shook hands as Rob laughed. "I can't afford your art, Joe. Books sell for a helluva lot less than one of your paintings."

"These are beautiful." I stood in awe before a watercolor of two little boys sitting on the beach playing in the sand. "I envy your talent."

"Now see, someone who appreciates me." Joe smiled.

"That's only because she doesn't know you as well as I do."

The guys continued chatting about the weather and the fishing as I wandered around the gallery. I would love to have one of his paintings. The colors were vibrant, bringing the scenes to life and reminding me of everything I'd seen since coming to the Cape. But while Rob might be jesting about affording one, I knew it would be awhile before I could.

"BJ?" Rob waved me over. "I was telling Joe about your house."

"I can't believe you rented that house," Joe said.

"I hear that a lot." I grimaced slightly.

"Anything weird happen yet?" he continued.

I thought about the storm. I was sure, in the light of day, I had overreacted. "Just a bunch of noise during the storm. I think it was branches banging against the house."

"Oh." Joe sounded disappointed.

"That's what previous renters would say. But they still left quickly," Rob commented.

"How come you two know about the house, yet you don't know it at all?"

Joe's brows bent over his nose as he studied me.

"Jeez, she talks in circles like you, Garrett."

"I'm serious. Everyone says there's something weird going on or that it's haunted, but nobody knows what or why. Or at least they're not telling me."

"I doubt that anyone knows," Rob said, "but that's why we're here. This building is believed to be one of the oldest buildings in P'town, although you wouldn't know it to look at it since it's been remodeled several times over the years. Still, there's rumors it's one of the original floated houses."

"Floated houses?" I recalled the way the floor at the cottage seemed to tilt under my feet during the storm. I looked down at the rough flooring and paused in thought. Nothing seemed to be moving.

"Have you been to Long Point?" The artist asked.

I shook my head.

He snorted. "Well, besides the fact you have a rotten tour guide, it's something you should see. It was built on the very end of the Cape in, hmm, 1816, when nothing else was out there. Within a few years, several families built homes there and they had a school and salt works."

"Wow," I said, "but there's nothing out there now except the lighthouse, right?"

"That's because," Rob said, "the houses were floated across the harbor to the mainland in the early 1860's."

I looked from one guy to the other. "This is all a big joke right? Because I'm a tourist?"

"No, honest," Rob replied. "I'd tell you to go research it, but I don't know that there's a lot written about them. However, there are several on the west end of town.”

“1860’s. I can’t believe they would have the wherewithal to do that. Why did they move to the inland side of the harbor?” I asked, intrigued.

“Some say for protection during the Civil War. Being on the outer curve of the cape made them vulnerable,” Joe said. “Others claim it had to do with the supply of wood and fresh water.”

“But what would make the difference if my cottage was a floated house? Why would that make it haunted? If it really is,” I added quickly.

Rob looked at me. “Hey, you’re the writer. I’m just helping with the research.”

“Aha,” Joe said, “no wonder she likes my paintings. Unlike you, she’s a creative soul.”

I smiled at his comment, but I was stuck on the idea that I might be living in a real piece of history. “You said there were more of these floated houses? Where? Anything close by?”

“Not close to me,” Joe said. “For some mysterious reason, this is the only one on this end of town, but there are more on the west end.”

I turned to Rob but before I could ask, he had my hand and was headed for the door.

“I assume I need to find a fifth for our weekly card game?” Joe asked as we were leaving. “Appears you’ll be busy doing research.”

"Rob, I can find my way around town if you have plans," I said.

He looked at me like I had said something totally crazy. "Why would I want to spend an evening with a guy that looked like him if I could spend it with you instead?"

I had absolutely no answer for that, so he steered me to the car, opened the door and gently nudged me onto the seat.

I could certainly get used to him, I thought, as he drove down Bradford Street. Although Commercial Street went from one end of P'town to the other, it usually had too many pedestrians and it was easier to drive on a parallel street. Once we got to Franklin, Rob turned left, cruised past Tremont, then the road curved right and we were at the West End back on Commercial Street. He slowed to a crawl, looking at the houses on both sides of the street. I didn't know what I was looking for, but suddenly he braked the car and pulled to the side of the road.

"There." He pointed to a two storied rectangular shaped house: two windows on each side of the door, upstairs and down. It had light tan siding and a neatly trimmed front yard with a flower garden full of hydrangeas.

"That doesn't look like my cottage at all. How do you know it's a floated house?"

"The plaque." He looked across the street. "There. That house has it above the door and this one has it in the corner." The second house was single story, more along the lines of the cottage.

The small blue and white ceramic plaque he referred to had a simple stick drawing of a house, curved along the base to represent a boat, sitting on waves. In the background was what I assumed to be Long Point lighthouse.

"So even if I can find a plaque, which I haven't noticed, how does that figure in with it being haunted?"

"Hey, I told you, you're—"

"I know, I'm the writer." And my brain was already running through scenarios. When was the cottage built or moved there? Why would people think it haunted? Just the noise?

"Do you suppose someone drowned when they moved it?" I asked.

"That's supposing it really is a floated house."

"Maybe someone drowned during a storm. That's why I heard noises last night, but not before then."

While we talked Rob slowly drove further down the street and I saw a few more houses with blue ceramic plaques. Those would be my first research stops.

By the time we arrived back at my place, the last vestiges of sunset glowed pink and orange on the horizon. Together we gathered supper ingredients, a couple of beers, and went out on the deck where Rob started the small gas grill.

"Why are you hooked on someone drowning?" he asked about my earlier suppositions.

I shrugged. "Maybe that's why the noise came during a storm." I sliced potatoes into a skillet that was heating at one end of the grill. "The only time I've heard noise was when it rained…"

"What noises exactly?"

"Thumping sounds, like they were coming from up-stairs."

Rob stepped to the back edge of the deck, looking along the roof and sides of the house. "Hey, you have a cupola."

"It's just for decoration. I can't find a way to get up there." I shrugged again. "It was probably just branches banging against it or the side of the house; the noise in the storm, I mean. Except for the 'yo'."

Rob's expression was incredible. First doubt, then wariness and consternation before his eyes crinkled at the corners and he broke into a grin. "Yo?"

"You don't have to believe me. That's just what it sounded like."

He reached around me to turn the steaks, and then put both arms around me from behind, propping his chin on my shoulder and swaying me back and forth as I tried to stir the potatoes. "Yo-ho-ho," he sang in my ear.

I could hear the laughter in his voice. I poked him with my elbow.

He let go of me but continued to laugh. "I want to be here next time."

Chapter 5
Research time

"Come to Boston with me," he said as we sat enjoying the late evening breeze after dinner.

"How long will you be gone?" A day trip on the ferry sounded like fun.

"Five days."

"I can't do that. I have—"

"To work," he finished for me. "You can't work all the time."

I turned my head and looked his way. The breeze played with his hair, causing a lock to fall over his forehead. I reached over and brushed it back, a completely unconscious gesture on my part. He smiled, grabbed my hand before I could remove it, and kissed my palm.

I could feel my face heat. Perhaps there was hope for me after all.

"Why are you going to Boston?" I prompted.

"A book fair."

I laughed, unable to stop. He looked at me, apparently unable to comprehend my merriment. When he finally realized what he had said, he joined me. "Okay, so sometimes a guy has to work, too. But you can do your job from anywhere; why not Boston?"

"You've made me curious about the origins of this cottage. I think researching here would be a lot more fun for now."

Since I had picked him up earlier that day, I drove him back to the bookstore although I teasingly threatened to make him walk. Before he got out of the car, he leaned over and kissed me; a light, lingering kiss that seemed more of a promise.

"I'll call you when I get back," he whispered. "Then we're going to talk."

He got out and closed the door before I could ask what he meant, although once I thought about it, I knew. I couldn't go forward, wherever that direction might take me, before I got rid of the past. Rob knew that and had been patiently prodding me. I dreaded that conversation yet realized nothing could happen—no forward progress toward the rest of my life—until I owned up to the past.

I spent the next day at Pilgrim's Monument, going through the exhibits and browsing the bookshelves. I couldn't find anything on the floating houses, except a short paragraph in their walking tour pamphlet.

I had just walked in the door of the cottage when my cell phone rang.

"Hey." Rob possessed one of those deep, smoky voices that felt like a caress, even when he just said 'hey'.

"Hi there. Are you back already?"

"No, I told you I'd be gone five days."

"You also said you would call when you got back."

"Okay, so I'm calling because I miss you."

Still unused to his constant attention, I wasn't sure what to say. "That's nice." I cringed. Couldn't I come up with something better? He was so much better at this relationship thing than I was, but I was determined to learn. "I miss you, too."

There was a long pause and I looked at my phone to make sure we were still connected. Cell reliability was notoriously poor out here. I almost missed his reply as I put the phone back to my ear.

"That's very nice."

I grinned, feeling like I had taken a huge step, although it was probably just a little shuffle.

"So did you work today like you said you would?"

"Actually, I did, but I didn't find anything more about floating houses than we already knew, and nothing about this particular one. But get this—did you know people who lived in this area were often given seafaring names like Oceanus? And John Cook's wife's middle name was Fish?"

"I knew that," he replied.

I had temporarily forgotten Rob lived here much longer than I and being a bookseller, he had probably read the Cape's history until he knew it by heart.

"Maybe I should just use you for research."

"That can be arranged. Do you read research in bed?"

"You could only wish," I replied but after I hung up, his question dangled at the forefront of my mind like a carrot before a rabbit.

* * *

I visited with some of the owners of floated houses the next day, but except for the original owner's names, all of whom were long dead, they couldn't offer much I didn't already know. After all, it was over one-hundred-sixty years ago, and a lot of the original history had been oral, now lost in time. When all else fails, there's a public library in almost any town, regardless of size, so I spent the afternoon sifting through an old card catalog and looking up books. In this case, library didn't necessarily mean automated.

Later in the week, I took a ride out to Long Point lighthouse on the Flyer ferry, enjoying our boat pilot's commentary. He knew about everything from lobster beds to the incredible, larger than life portraits of several old women at the end of Fisherman's Wharf. The subjects of the pictures appeared ageless, representing past inhabitants of the area and symbolizing all the attributes of sturdy ancestors.

Troy dropped us off on the beach near the very tip of the cape, promising to come back in a few hours. I enjoyed walking on the beach. The sand felt warm beneath my feet, but the water was cool as it splashed onto the shore. The crystalline blue sky and the vast ocean met at the horizon with barely any distinction in color, making me feel as though I were inside a huge blue ball.

The tide was rising, and I stood still, letting the waves wash past me, each a little further up the shore than the one before. Every time they receded, pebbles bounced off my ankles as they tumbled by, and the water took some of the sand beneath my feet. I closed my eyes and used my other senses to soak up the day. The overriding sense of swaying, like I was on a boat as it rode the waves, caught me unaware, and I held my arms out to balance. The constant rhythm of the waves and the soft breeze across the water produced a gentle peace I wanted to grab with both hands and stuff in my pockets to keep.

As I sucked in another breath of clean, sweet air, I realized that everything I was feeling was already mine and I didn't need to hide it away for fear of losing it. I opened my eyes and turned slowly in a complete circle, seeing things a little differently. The waves and shore were in total harmony. Even as the water washed away grains of sand, it deposited more in their stead. The sun in all its heated glory colored the sky with light, and the water in turn reflected back those rays, like millions of fireflies dancing on the surface.

"I can do this," I whispered on the breeze. "I can find peace, live in harmony, and give back to those who want to share my life." My voice rose as I looked skyward. "I am a terrific person and I have a lot to give."

My phone rang as if in applause for the incredible—for me—epiphany I was having. I looked at the caller ID and smiled.

"Hi, I really miss you."

"Knock me over with a feather," Rob breathed softly. "Damn, because I was calling to say I have to stay an extra day."

I felt a stab of disappointment. It wasn't like I was ready to jump into bed with him, but I was ready to take a step forward. "Well, double damn."

"You must have had a great day researching, to feel so magnanimous."

"Actually, I know little more about the house than I did yesterday," I said. But I know a whole lot more about myself. "I got a printout from the library of part of the History of Barnstable County, Massachusetts, copyright 1890, that I'm trying to wade through."

"All of it? That thing is thousands of pages long."

"I should have known you would have heard of it."

"Honey, I'm a bookseller. Of course I knew that." I could hear the teasing in his voice, referring to yesterday's conversation.

"Did you know the buoys on lobster traps are different colors and patterns to represent different families or companies?" I asked, recalling what Troy had recounted while we crossed the harbor.

"Yeah, I knew that, too."

"Okay, did you know that if a man speaks at sea where no woman can hear, he's still wrong?"

He laughed. "I hadn't heard that bit of research. Did one of the wise women at the end of the pier say that?" He was referring to the portraits I had seen at Fisherman's Wharf called They Also Faced the Sea of five courageous women who represented the very backbone of the original Portuguese fishing village.

"I've learned from them, too, this week." I thought about the information I had read—how they were resilient through good times and bad and made of strength and courage.

"From them?"

"Yes, from what was said about them," I replied. "But the saying about the man at sea was just something I saw on a plaque."

"Am I going to find it on the wall in your kitchen the next time I come out?"

This time I laughed. "No, but if I find one that says, 'I knew that', I'll get it for you."

By the end of the week, I had concluded that my cottage was just your run-of-the-mill cottage and not an historic floated house. That was okay by me. Since I didn't own it there was no reason to get excited about its significance. In fact, had it any history to speak of, it probably wouldn't have been empty, regardless of what people said about it being haunted.

Through my reading, however, I had become fascinated with the history and lore of the Cape and thought about writing a story set here. With that in mind, I spread the information I had out on the kitchen table and tried to construct a timeline of important details.

Both the lighthouse at Long Point and Race Point were constructed in 1816, but the Race Point was a revolving light to differentiate it from the others. It wasn't until 1872 that the government built the Wood End light, which sat between the other two on the long curve of the peninsula. It was interesting that while all the lights were automated, Race Point still had a Keeper, because there had been several mechanical glitches throughout the years when the light would mysteriously go out. That wasn't ideal if there was a storm or fog because of the treacherous sand bars all along the outer bank.

"Speaking of," I muttered as the lights flickered. Dark clouds had banked, then dissipated throughout the day, causing the air to be heavy and muggy. I knew another storm was brewing and Rob wasn't due back until tomorrow on the afternoon ferry. It wasn't that I was frightened, exactly, but now as I stepped out on the deck, the sky had turned yellow greenish, and I hoped it would blow out to sea rather than scallop along the coast.

I flipped the switch to the small, battery-operated radio I purchased after the last storm. The music was full of static and continually cutting in and out, but no one interrupted with storm warnings. I looked at my research still spread across the table, thinking I should get back to it, but I'd been sitting in that chair most of the day and I needed to do something more physical.

Another peek outside made me reconsider taking a walk on the beach. I went through the fridge and cupboards, pulling out ingredients to make bread. Without a cookbook, which certainly hadn't been in the box of research books I had brought with me, I would have to rely on my memory, and the only recipe I vividly recalled was for round loaves of raisin bread. It had been one of those recipes I cut out of the paper years ago and made often because it was quick, even though it called for yeast.

I measured all the dry ingredients into a large bowl and put the water on the stove to heat. I had no sooner clicked the knob to medium high when thunder rumbled outside, and the lights flickered.

My chin hit my chest in defeat. "Not again," I muttered. Night had already fallen so the kitchen was totally dark. I felt my way along the counter then reached across to the table. One thing about the electricity often failing was I had developed the habit of leaving things in the same spot at the end of a storm. I knew exactly where the lanterns, candles, and matches were each time.

Thump, thump.

My gaze automatically went to the ceiling, even though the noise sounded more like it came from the living room.

"Where's the 'yo'?" I asked, but not loudly, half afraid someone—or something—would actually answer. Instead, there was a flash of lightning and a distant rumble. Maybe my wish would be granted, and the storm would track out to sea.

I looked forlornly at where my bread bowl sat on the counter. My cell phone rang, and I picked it up, absently thinking of the coarse texture of that raisin bread and how great it tasted with melted butter. My stomach growled just as I said hello.

"What was that? I heard something. Crap, I can't believe I promised you I would be there for the next storm, and I'm stuck in Boston." Rob sounded almost frantic.

"Rob, calm down. It's okay." My stomach growled again.

"Bonnie Jo, what the hell was that?"

He had never called me by my full name, and it startled me that he was that concerned. At the same time, his concern and my stomach had me laughing at the absurdity of it all.

"What you hear is not a ghost. I was in the middle of making raisin bread and the electricity went out. Now my stomach is protesting the tease."

I heard him sigh with relief just before lightning cracked much closer and my phone went dead.

There wasn't anything to do but go to bed and hopefully sleep through it. I blew out all the candles except the gold lantern, which would give me enough light to see my way to the loft. Making sure the doors were locked, I walked down the hall, sliding one hand along the wall to guide me. I refused to look at the portrait on the door as I went through, even though I told myself there were no eyes looking back at me.

* * * *

Hours later, I shot straight up in bed, frantically willing my heart to stay in my chest. The room was pitch black and thunder shook the entire cottage, making it feel as though it were rolling on the swells of the ocean. I grabbed the edge of the bed as my stomach pitched. Was it just the storm that had awakened me?

Thump, thump. *"Yo! Move quickly ye scabs!"*

I screamed as lightning flashed, illuminating dark shadows moving across the end of my bed. I scooted up against the headboard. My ears were ringing, the sounds of the storm echoing inside my head as well as outside the cottage. I felt like I was drowning, unable to breathe and as hard as I tried, I couldn't move.

More lightning crashed. In the shadows, defined by the brief spurt of light, was the shape of a man in a dark flowing cloak leaning over my bed.

"Rob?" I practically cried in relief, just before something icy cold and wet brushed across my face and neck.

"To starboard!"

Screaming, I tumbled from bed, the covers twisting around my legs and tripping me. I fell hard on the floor, my knees and palms stinging from the slide against wood. I kicked and clawed my way out of the tangle, crying as I scrambled to the stairs at the other end of the loft. Even when lightning cracked again I didn't look back, petrified at what I might see.

I just wanted out!

Thunder rumbled and the cottage swayed, making it almost impossible to go down the narrow stairs. I knew my eyes were open, but I couldn't see a thing. Instead of feeling my way carefully with my feet, I moved too quickly and missed the last step before the small turn. My head banged against the door, and I slumped onto the bottom step.

I tried talking to myself to calm my fears. "You know there's nothing up there. It's just the wind and the lightning and the thunder making all those sounds and shadows."

The terrified part of my brain countered that those sounds were words—words!—not some wind moaning in the trees.

I put my hands to my ears, trying to block out the noise, but the wind had risen to a fever pitch, buffeting the cottage while the rain continued to pound the roof. I reached for the doorknob, but it wouldn't turn beneath my hand. I stood, twisting and turning it as I shoved my shoulder against the wood. It didn't have a lock; I knew it didn't, so why wouldn't it open? What was blocking it on the other side?

I dropped back onto the step. My hands stung from my fall and from trying to open the door. My knees were burning and shaking so hard they knocked together. The only thing on the other side of the door was that damned portrait. If it had fallen in the storm, it could well be jammed against the doorknob, preventing my escape.

I jumped up and spun around when a horrendous crash and breaking glass sounded from above. Had the entire roof caved in? Did I dare venture back up the stairs? Lightning no longer flashed so I wasn't sure what I could see. Besides, what about the shadows and the words?

It was long minutes later before I realized the only sounds I heard were the thumping of my own heart and my heavy breathing. I closed my mouth and breathed through my nose, concentrating on that and not the fear that still swept through me. As hard as I listened, I couldn't hear anything, not even rain. I collapsed on the bottom step, crying, this time because I had survived the night, and whatever had come after me in the storm.

Chapter 6
The Aftermath

An echo of sound intruded on my consciousness, and I stiffened, ready to be attacked from behind.

Thump, thump!

My foggy brain couldn't make sense of the words being yelled, but I did recognize the thump of heavy boots on the hardwood. I held my breath as the door to the stairway was flung wide.

I screamed, then screamed again as a figure in a long rain slicker reached for me. I fought against the strong hands that grabbed me.

"Shh, baby, I've got you." Rob took a step into the stairway.

"No!" I threw myself at him, toppling us both into the hall. He managed to keep his balance while I wrapped my arms around his neck and hung on for dear life. "Don't go in there." I started crying, deathly afraid that Rob would get hurt by the monster that might still be lurking upstairs.

He untangled my arms and grabbed my hands to pull me down the hall. I cried out. He looked down at my scraped hands.

"Holy sh...what the hell happened?" He scooped me up and carried me away from the stairway, out into the bright light of the kitchen.

"It's morning?" I squinted against the sunlight pouring through the windows. "You weren't supposed to be back until this afternoon."

"When I heard how bad they predicted the storm to be and I couldn't reach you on your cell, I rented a car."

"Oh, Rob, you didn't have to do that. That's expensive, and how will you get the car back? Besides, driving in the rain is dangerous. What if you had been in an accident?" I was babbling but couldn't seem to stop.

He squatted in front of me, his face so dear even as he scowled that I leaned forward and kissed him. His lips were hot and firm against mine, and when he put his warm hands on my shoulders to steady himself, uncontrollable shivers raced through me. My teeth began chattering and my hands shook.

"What a time for you to get romantic," he muttered as he pulled away. "Sweetheart, I've got to get you warmed up." He stood but I grabbed his hand, wincing as my own palm began bleeding when I curled my hand around his wrist.

"I...saw...it," I stammered. "The g...ghost."

He shifted his gaze to the window, and I saw his brow furrow as he stared at something outside. When he turned back to me, his eyes were intense, dark gray in the morning light. "I think we need to get you to a doctor."

"I swear I'm not hallucinating. I saw it!"

"BJ, I'm not just talking about whatever happened last night. Look at you—your hands are cut, your knees are scraped, and you're shaking like a leaf in a storm."

I winced at the word.

"Sorry. It's just that you're a mess."

I snorted, as much of a laugh as I could manage. "Gee, thanks, it's good to see you, too."

He came back and knelt in front of me again. "You know what I mean. You need medical attention."

"I'll be okay, now that you're here. And if you make me some coffee." I gave him a weak smile.

And I was. Just knowing he was here, and that it was daylight, chased the shadows away. When he turned toward the counter, I stood, wobbled a little, but managed to hobble to the bathroom where I brushed my teeth and combed my hair, splashed water on my face, and grabbed some first aid medicine.

Rob met me in the hall, his face white. "Geez, I turn my back for a second and you disappear. I thought you'd gone back upstairs."

"Well, eventually I will. Something crashed last night, and I need to find out what the damage is." The thought of going back up there had my stomach in knots. I crunched up my mouth. "Maybe you could go up there?"

"Just because I'm a guy, I'm supposed to be brave?"

"Yes?"

He sighed. "Coffee first. I hear bravery is enhanced with caffeine."

He poured two large mugs, added creamer, and brought me one. As I sipped the extra strong brew, he wet a dish towel with warm water, kneeling before me and gently washing my knees, which were scraped almost as badly as my hands. He applied some cream to both knees then my palms.

"I fell out of bed," I said by way of explanation. When he lifted a brow, I added, "My feet got twisted in the sheet. But Rob, someone was up there, yelling at me, telling me to hurry; to go to starboard."

He looked as if he didn't quite believe me. "You have a nautical ghost giving you directions in the height of a storm?"

"The thing is, when I managed to get to the bottom of the stairs, the door was jammed. I couldn't get out."

Now he shook his head. "There was nothing jamming it. I opened it right up."

"It was locked; I know it was." I shivered again. "What's going on?"

"Let's look outside and see if there's any structural damage. The wind was a son of a gun last night."

I refilled my coffee and slipped into my Crocs as Rob opened the back door. I had no sooner stepped onto the deck than I heard him swear.

"It looks like a branch went through your roof." He pointed to a spot on the back side where I could easily see a branch sticking out from where a skylight used to be. "That could account for the noise you heard."

"Damn it, Rob, I heard the noises—the voice—before that branch crashed down." As scared as I was last night, now I was mad that he didn't believe me.

"Look, all I'm saying is—"

"You don't believe me." I turned on my heel and went inside, letting the door slam. He was right behind me.

"Let's just see what the damage is. You'll need to call the realtor and have someone come out." He set his coffee cup on the counter and walked through the left archway to the hall. "We never get this kind of weather on the Cape, but the way this summer is going; there could be another storm any time."

"Man, I hope not." My words were faint, but he instantly turned and pulled me into his arms.

"I know you had to be scared to death. And I promised to be here, and I wasn't. I'm sorry."

I reached up and kissed his chin. "Shh, remember you said friends don't have to say they're sorry."

He chuckled. "We sound like an old movie. Come on; let's see what the damage is." He was halfway down the hall when I suddenly realized where he was going.

"Wait." I grabbed his tee shirt at the back and tugged. He stopped.

"What?" He half turned toward me.

"It's my...bedroom."

His eyes glittered and his lips turned up into a wolfish grin. "Why don't you want me in your bedroom?"

The reasons were many, and I didn't want something to happen between us just because I was still high on adrenaline from last night. But the first thing that popped out of my mouth was, "I'm a slob."

He laughed. "That's not the reason and you know it. I thought we weren't going to lie to each other. Besides, if I was going to make love to you, I wouldn't necessarily need a bedroom."

"Oh." Disappointment sat like a rock in my stomach.

He turned completely around, tipping my chin up with a finger. "I didn't say I didn't want to. I just said we wouldn't necessarily need a bed."

"Oh." This time the feeling was more like butterflies.

He just shook his head, taking my wrist and tugging me behind him up the narrow stairs. When he was close to the top, where his head was floor level, he stopped.

"Son of a bitch."

My stomach did a free fall. Even with my vivid imagination, I couldn't envision what he was seeing and being several steps below, I couldn't see.

"What?" I squeaked.

"Wait here." He let go of my hand and took the remaining steps two at a time. I heard his boots clump across the hardwood floor, reminding me of the sounds I had heard last night. Scrambling up the stairs, I didn't wait for him to call me.

I came to a dead stop not a foot from the stairs, my head spinning and the floor tilting crazily. I grabbed the railing just as Rob reached me to keep me from tumbling back down the stairs. Together we stared at the damage from last night's storm. It wasn't the huge tree branch shooting through the roof where the skylight had been that made my knees shake and my heart pound. It was the fact that my bed—where I had been sleeping just hours ago—was pierced clear through by the jagged edges of wood from the tree and shards of glass from the windows.

I sucked in a breath. No ghost had done this. The wickedness of the storm sank in, and I shivered. It was one thing to hear it in the dead of night, but another to see the evidence of its fury and to think I could have been in that bed.

"You could have been..." Rob couldn't voice the terror and I couldn't grasp it.

"No, I was on the stairs when I heard the crash."

"You were in the bed."

"No, I wasn't; I'm sure." My mind couldn't comprehend the possibility. "No, you're wrong."

Rob looked at me long and hard, started to say something then stopped.

"What?" I asked.

He shook his head. "Never mind. Where's a bag? We'll grab you some clothes and go to my place. You can't stay here until they get that fixed."

I started giggling uncontrollably, tears streaming down my cheeks. If I wasn't so focused on what he had said, I would realize I was bordering on hysteria.

"Bonnie, look at me." He grabbed my upper arms and shook me slightly. I sobered but still felt bubbles of laughter inside.

"I know what you're thinking, but I'm not hysterical. I just realized how often we use the word 'that' for all those things we don't want to discuss. We haven't talked about 'that' —my relationship with my ex-husband. Now we won't mention 'that'," I nodded toward the bed, "because if we discuss it, we'd have to admit I could have died last night."

He hugged me tight, kissing the top of my head. "You're nuts, you know it?" He kept kissing me like he couldn't get enough. His hands splayed across my back, and I felt a slight tremor in his touch. The thought of death did tend to raise one's passions to the surface, I thought, as his lips left a warm path down my temple and across my cheek until he found my lips. It wasn't a kiss of passion, though I felt it bubbling up inside me, warming me and making me realize I held a special place in Rob's heart.

When he finally released me, I tilted my head back and captured his clear gray gaze. "Now that, we can discuss all day long."

He kissed my nose. "Man, I missed your sassy mouth."

I pouted. "Yes, you just did."

He laughed. "No more until we get you somewhere safe." As if in response to his words, the branch behind us creaked and shifted, dropping a little further through the roof.

* * *

By the time I packed, and we headed for town, I felt exhausted. Aftershocks, I thought, leaning my head back and closing my eyes. I didn't wake up until Rob slammed the car door, muttering as he started the car.

I sat up and looked around, realizing we were at the realtor's office. "What happened?"

"Stupid people around here. Henrietta said it would take a while to find someone who would be willing to work out there. I told her if she'd quit spreading rumors about the place, maybe she could sell it."

"Oh, Rob, maybe she thought saying it was haunted would raise its appeal."

"You are just too nice, you know it?"

"Of course, I am." I gave him a smile. "But I'm also totally exhausted. I don't think I slept at all last..." I let out a big yawn before continuing. "Last night during the storm." I reminded myself I was taking steps forward, and that meant getting past fears of all kinds.

He put the car in gear and pulled out onto Bradford Street before taking a left at Pearl.

"Aren't you going to the bookstore?"

"Not until I have you warm and dry in my...in a bed."

I wondered if he felt it, too. Without our knowing it, and perhaps as a result of the storm and near disaster, our relationship had taken several steps all by itself and now we were scrambling to catch up. It was a nice feeling to be open to the surprise of what might happen next.

* * *

Rob's house was so typically male, so him, that I felt instantly at home. The furniture was overstuffed and in warm tones and piles of books were everywhere. It was a busy place, but not really cluttered.

"I thought the bookstore was downtown," I teased as he swept a batch of magazines off a chair.

"I wasn't expecting company."

"If it's too much trouble, I can find a room... somewhere." I didn't want to find a room, really, I wanted to stay here. More aftershocks, I told myself. I yawned, not getting it covered with my hand before he noticed.

"You need a warm bath and sleep. I can go to the store once you're settled." He led me down a short hall, opening a door on the right as he passed. "Bathroom." He dropped my bag on the floor by that door as he continued. The last door on the left was his bedroom, as warm and comfortable as he was and unlike the living room, everything was in its place. The bed was even made. "You can sleep here. I'll use the couch."

"You really don't have to, you know," I said rather shyly. At his look, I stammered, "Give me your bed, that is." I mentally shook my head. I was making such a botch of it.

He put his hands on my shoulders and ducked his head until he filled my vision. "We'll get it figured out. It's not something to be forced, so don't try so hard." He kissed my forehead, turned me around and gave me a slight push. "Into a warm bath now."

* * *

It was late afternoon by the time I woke, and I could barely get out of bed. My hands and knees hurt, I had a headache, and my eyes felt like sandpaper. I lifted my legs straight out in front of me and looked at the sorry sight of my knees, still oozing a little even though Rob put ointment on them before I climbed into bed. My hands were a little better, the heels looking mostly like rug burns.

When I felt I could walk without falling down, I wandered to the kitchen to find a note on the table.

Will be home about five with carryout. You are to rest and do not (underline, underline) pick up my mess.

I smiled. I suppose under normal circumstances I would have puttered around stacking magazines and straightening, but my knees were sore enough that I could hardly bend. I looked over at the stove clock to see it was already after four, so I supposed I should get dressed.

I just finished brushing my teeth when I heard Rob come in. One look at his face when I met him in the kitchen, and I knew something was wrong.

At first he wouldn't say anything when I asked. He just kept scowling and grumbling until I finally tapped him on the shoulder and when he turned around, I kissed him. I surprised myself by taking the initiative, but he quickly took over, gently pulling me into a hug. A very long minute, or two, later he set me away and started pulling boxes from the bag he had brought in.

"I went out to the cottage and picked up your papers and computer," he said.

"Thank you. That was very thoughtful." I looked down at my hands. "I'm not sure I'm ready to use it, but maybe I can get through more of that history of Barnstable County."

"Actually, I wanted to take a little more time and look at the damage. I think that tree went through at the sky light, instead of a separate section of roof, which may make it a lot easier to repair."

"That would be good," I replied cautiously. His tone of voice indicated there was more that he wasn't saying.

He brought steaming bowls of clam chowder over to the table where I sat. He went back and poured two glasses of water, grabbed a small loaf of French bread and the butter, and set them in the middle before he sat down.

"Here, eat while it's hot."

"Are you going to tell me what it is you don't want to tell me?" Usually when I talked in doubles, he'd laugh, but this time he frowned, though not as fiercely as earlier. He ate half a bowl of chowder before he spoke.

"A couple of the front windows were broken, too, probably from the wind, and glass was scattered all across the floor in the living room. That's another reason I brought in your computer. I found a couple of boards and nailed them across the breaks, but it won't stop someone intent on getting in to steal something."

"My computer's the only thing worth stealing, so it doesn't matter now."

"Tell me again what you think happened last night."

I scowled at him. "It's not what I think; it's what I know."

"Well, sometimes things get a little out of proportion in the midst of traumatic circumstances."

"Oh, you're a psychologist now?" I wasn't really mad at him because I knew he was right. At least this time I coaxed a smile out of him.

"Just humor me, would you?" He leaned back in his chair, stretching his legs under the table. His foot brushed mine and instead of moving it off, he rubbed both of his sock clad feet over mine.

"The electricity went out, so I figured there was nothing to do but go to bed." I wiggled my toes against the soles of his feet, just to let him know I liked the contact. "I woke up to someone yelling at me and when I realized it wasn't you, I panicked and fell out of bed, banging my hands and knees."

His frown deepened. "Do you remember what you thought this person was yelling?"

I decided to ignore his continued reference to *what I thought,* like I only imagined it. "I distinctly heard a man's voice yelling at me to hurry. In fact, he said 'move quickly ye scabs' and then 'to starboard'."

Rob looked at me like he wasn't seeing me at all but something beyond my shoulder. I turned quickly but of course nothing was there. "Then what?"

"I scrambled down the stairs but couldn't get out the door. Then you found me. End of story." I raised my brows and just looked at him, waiting for some explanation I was sure he would give. When he didn't say anything for a minute or two, my mind began going back over the details. Had there been something else? I closed my eyes and tried to see into the darkness that had surrounded me last night, but all I could remember was the shadow of a man who wasn't Rob, a voice that was deep and raspy and kept yelling at me to hurry and to...

"Holy mackerel."

"What? Is there something else?" Rob leaned forward, reaching across to grab my trembling hands.

"He was warning me," I whispered.

"What are you talking about?" Warm hands squeezed mine, the pressure grounding me, but my heart still pounded, and my ears were ringing. I looked across the short distance, not seeing Rob at all but instead the dark shadowy figure.

"He told me to hurry, but then I couldn't get out the door downstairs. If I had stayed in bed the tree would have killed me." I gasped for breath; my thoughts suddenly crystal clear. "And if I had gotten out the door and into the living room, the flying glass from the windows might have killed me, too."

"Bonnie." He tilted his head, and his voice held a note of annoyance, like he knew what I was thinking and didn't want me to say it out loud.

"Rob, don't you see? That ghost saved my life!"

Chapter 7
Discovery

I woke up screaming, the nightmare so vivid I grabbed the edge of the bed to try and stop the pitch and roll I felt beneath me. I was drenched in sweat, feeling like I had been splashed with water; like a huge wave hit me broadside and I floundered on the brink of something dangerous.

A hand touched me, and I screamed again, flinging out my arms to ward off being captured.

"Bonnie." The hands were rough now, grabbing my shoulders to hold me still. As hard as I tried, I couldn't struggle up from the depths of the fear that gripped me. "Bonnie Jo, wake up!"

I bolted upright, looking wildly around, my eyes not focusing in the dim light. Even when I began to see shapes and shadows, I couldn't tell where I was. A soothing voice came to me and for an instant I thought it was the voice in my dream telling me to hurry. I swung my legs over the edge of the bed but was grabbed from behind and held close.

"Stop struggling. I've got you and I won't let anything hurt you." The voice continued speaking softly in my ear and I gradually realized it was Rob. I collapsed against his chest, sobbing from the unknown terror that engulfed me.

My heart continued to pound even when Rob climbed onto the bed and pulled me closer. I stiffened reflexively.

I heard him sigh, his breath tickling the back of my neck just before he kissed me there. "You're like a wild filly I have to tame."

I knew he was trying to take my mind off my nightmare, and I did appreciate his efforts. His hand gently touched my shoulder, and I could feel him from back to buttocks as he curled along my back. His chest brushed my back as he breathed, slow and steady.

"You grew up in Boston," I said. "How many wild fillies have you ever tamed?"

Another soft kiss on my shoulder. Like a hot brand through the light fabric of my tee shirt. "None," he said softly, "and I find the experience exhilarating."

I smiled in the dark, relaxing further against him. The last remnants of the nightmare faded away, leaving me with an uneasy feeling but no specific details about what it had been about. Or maybe my unease had to do more with a man in my bed—or me in his to be exact—because it had been such a long time, and I really didn't know what to expect or how I would react.

"Making love and having sex aren't the same, you know." His whispered words banged against the shield I erected so many long months ago, denting it in several places.

Rob had the uncanny ability to read my moods, if not my thoughts. He didn't push, didn't pry, and as a result I opened up with my feelings. And when I did, regardless of what they were, he didn't judge.

"The two are nowhere near close. Trust me?" His arm came around my waist and his hand flattened against my stomach, but it didn't move beyond that. He was waiting and I was panicking.

Trust. That single word that meant everything in a relationship and that which I had so little left of in my heart. Could I? I had come to realize I had a lot to gain by knowing Rob; a lot I could learn. But there was also so much to lose if he betrayed me. He didn't even know all my reasons for being here, or my history, and yet he gave to me without asking anything in return. He trusted me.

"Yes," I said, "I do trust you."

His arm tightened around me. "Good," he said and grew still. It was several minutes later that I realized he had fallen asleep.

I had to admit I was disappointed.

* * *

My hands didn't hurt quite so much the next morning, so after a quick shower, I spread my research out on Rob's kitchen table and grabbed a cup of coffee. I had pretty much eliminated the idea of my rented cottage being a floated house, so now I wasn't sure what I was looking for. Regardless, in order to solve the puzzle of who—or what—was haunting the place, I would have to do a lot of reading and looking at the history of P'town.

I was still trying to wade through the meanings of some old-fashioned words in the printed history when Rob noisily entered through the back door. I really should feel guilty about taking him away from his business, but he didn't seem to mind, and I was beginning to like the attention. He put me first.

"I figured after last night you might sleep in," he said.

I looked at him across the width of the table. "Which part of last night?"

He actually blushed, even though we hadn't done anything, and I woke up alone. But I certainly hadn't forgotten the feel of his body against mine, the sound of his breathing, the touch of his lips and his hands.

"You don't remember the nightmare?"

I shook my head. "I recall being scared to death, but I'm not sure from what." I looked shyly up at him. "I do remember you climbing into bed with me."

This time he grinned widely, reaching across the table to place a long, brown paper-wrapped package on top of my papers. "This is for you." He turned and grabbed a cup of coffee before sitting across from me.

I tore off the brown paper to find a tole-painted plaque. The writing was upside down, so I flipped it over, reading out loud, "It's never too late to live happily ever after." I looked over at Rob. "I like that. It's definitely words to live by, even if it's hard to do some days."

"Why?"

"Sometimes I think I need one that says, 'you are not guilty'."

"For what?"

I sighed. "All the wrongs in my life."

"Are you ready to tell me about that?"

"Are you ready for tears, anger, and remorse?" I moved to the counter for the coffeepot. "Oh, and probably a lot of swearing."

He came up behind me and put an arm around my waist. "I've got broad shoulders and I think there was a sailor somewhere in my ancestry. Come on; let's go out on the deck."

Funny how even when I was trying so hard to be different, I fell quickly into a routine. I took the lounge just like I did at the cottage, and Rob took the chair, propping his feet on the railing.

He took a sip of coffee then glanced at me before turning his gaze back beyond the railing. His house wasn't that far from the harbor, but sound was muted by the foliage surrounding us. The silence between us grew louder, but for some reason not uncomfortable.

I closed my eyes, letting my surroundings seep into my senses: the smell of the salt air, the soothing sounds of birds in the distance, the gentle caress of the breeze.

"You asleep?" His voice teased.

"Maybe I'm not ready. Maybe I need…"

"BJ, it's whatever you want. I won't push you. But can I give you a little advice?"

"Can I stop you?" I opened one eye and peered at him.

He grinned, and then slowly sobered again. "You'll never be able to move forward if you don't let go of the past."

The really nice thing about being friends was we could always speak our minds and allow the other person the same right. When I was married, I would seldom say what I thought for fear of making my husband mad. Even if I knew I was right. When I did speak out and we argued, I would always end up saying I was sorry.

The really not so nice thing about being friends and saying what we thought is that although the words weren't hurtful, they were truthful, which was sometimes harder to take.

"The guilt I spoke of? What did I do wrong that made him turn elsewhere?"

"I know what you're going through."

I turned and looked at him. "No, you don't. My husband had an affair. Your wife died."

The silence was profound. I had overstepped the boundaries of friendship.

"I felt all the same things you do, for different reasons," he whispered, the sadness of his features tearing at my heart. "You said you felt guilty because your husband looked elsewhere. Well, the guilt's not just yours. I felt it because I was alive, and she wasn't. I wasn't good enough for her so God took her away. You might wonder how you could compete with another woman. Let me ask you, how do you compete with God?"

I reached over and touched his arm, and he put a hand over mine. He didn't push me away. "And yet you haven't lost your faith."

He laughed harshly. "Oh, I did. I was exactly where you are—the feelings of worthlessness because I couldn't fix what was wrong. Always saying I was sorry, even if it wasn't my fault. Then there was the shame because I wanted something I couldn't have—a loving responsive wife. It took awhile, but I finally decided I could lie down and die or continue to live." He looked me straight in the eye and added, "If you choose life, then you have to live like you mean it. You can't keep saying 'what if' and you can't look back. You have to make it count."

"He took away my dreams!" I practically shouted. Now that all stops were out, I couldn't seem to stem the flow of words.

"Didn't you have shared dreams?"

"Of course we did—our children, his career. I followed him with every change he made. I found jobs when we moved, even if they weren't in my field. I was always there, even doing the same things he did recreationally."

"But he wouldn't let you write?"

"Oh, he never said I couldn't, but he was never interested in what I wrote, and he never offered to help with other things if I was in the middle of a story. Even the Christmas stories I wrote for friends didn't get read. I didn't hide what I wrote, it was all there on the computer. He apparently read something because when I first accused him of having an affair, he accused me of going out and researching my plots, specifically the sex."

"He accused you because he was doing it."

"That's about it. And he said he didn't want me sharing it with the wives of his business associates. It was a reflection on him; apparently a bad one."

"I find your stories riveting."

"The sex?"

"No, not just the sex, although that does turn me on." He wiggled his eyebrows at me. "I have to wonder—"

"Don't you dare ask me where I learned it."

He just looked at me without saying a word.

I blushed. "Sorry, I always get defensive when it comes to my writing. The romance book industry as a whole takes a lot of flak, especially with all the erotica out there today. Nobody asks James Patterson if he really goes around killing people, so he knows how to write about murder."

He laughed. "I was going to say that I have to wonder why you stayed in that relationship so long."

I sighed. "It was the way I was raised. My parents weren't happy in their later years, but they stuck it out. And I would ask myself what I had to be unhappy about. He didn't beat me; he made good money, and we had a nice home and took vacations. Maybe at first it was for the kids. Then it was just the familiarity of where I was and the fear of the unknown. Moving out wasn't the least bit comfortable."

"Did you ever think about going back?"

"I did go back the first time I moved out, but not this last time. He hurt me too badly. It was one thing to have an affair, because it destroyed my trust, and he wasn't treating me with the respect I deserved as his wife. But he also lied about it, and even when he told me he would do anything to keep me from being so unhappy, he turned right around and saw her again. And because of his accusations about my writing, I felt ashamed of what I wrote. I didn't write for eight months after that."

"Tell me about your writing—how you decide what to write and the form it takes."

"See that's the thing. I don't always get to decide if it will be a romance, a suspense or mystery; very sexy or a little sexy. I get an idea—and they come from everywhere so don't ask me that—and I write. I started a story that I thought would be an erotica, but the characters weren't ready for a fast relationship; they wanted to take it nice and slow, so it ended up being a soft romance."

"You talk like your characters are real people."

I tilted my head and gave him a look. "Come on, Rob. I'm sure you've read a book so good you couldn't put it down. It drew you in and you felt you were part of the story?"

He nodded. "So as a writer, you sort of live your stories."

"I guess in a way that's right. And maybe that was what upset my husband. He thought I was writing my knight in shining armor, and he wasn't it. But I knew they were fiction. I didn't try to bring them to life; I didn't commit adultery by acting out my stories. To me, writing a good story is similar to watching a good movie. People watch to be entertained; they know the stories aren't true. I write to do the entertaining.

"Besides, there are plenty of romance authors who dedicate their books to their husbands who are the loves of their lives or are their own personal knights. So not every man has a problem with his wife writing sex."

"Personally, I think it would be fun to do some of what you write about."

"Exactly. That's what I told my ex. I said instead of thinking that's what I am doing, maybe he should think that's what I would like to do."

Rob didn't say anything; just looked at me. I suddenly realized how my comment sounded, and I could feel my face grow warm. He was reading my work. Did he think I wanted to do everything I had written about? I groaned, burying my face in my hands.

After a minute, I heard him clear his throat before he cautiously asked, "What are you working on now with all those papers on the table inside?"

"I'm curious about the cottage. There is something going on, whether you believe it or not, so right now I'm just trying to find out more about it. Maybe it'll lead to a story, maybe not."

I laughed. "I'm notorious for jotting down all sorts of things, thinking they'll develop into stories. I have a whole file of ideas, most of which will never see the light of day."

Rob stood. "Speaking of books and all that, Maxie said she could only work until noon, so I have to get back. Are you going to be okay here by yourself this afternoon? I can leave my car if you need it."

I shook my head. "I'll work on what I have available, maybe do some online research. If I do decide to go anywhere, I'll come down to the store."

"Don't think about going out to the cottage."

An involuntary shiver went through me. "I doubt I'm ready for that. I have no desire to run into the ghost. You know, I could write a ghost story about the cottage."

"I don't believe in ghosts."

"Yes, so you've said. But I'm telling you something talked to me, and something saved my life by getting me out of there. So maybe I'll write a something story." I smirked at him.

* * *

I ended up staying at Rob's a full week while workmen repaired the skylight and replaced the downstairs windows. Every night he kissed me good night, some kisses short and sweet and others lingering. I treasured the touches, the hugs, and the gentle caresses. He never seemed to be in a hurry, and his tender attention was dissolving my defenses.

Every night as I went to bed alone, I recalled what he said about living life to the fullest. He showed me in so many different ways that he cared, and I was beginning to give back because I now actually felt I had something to give.

134

I was healing, replenishing my spirit through my writing, the peace of the seashore, and the friendships I was developing. I didn't have to feel guilty for what I thought or wrote, and I had a dear friend in Rob who was helping, rather than demanding my time for himself. But was I ready to take the next step in a relationship?

One afternoon, I was in the kitchen when he came home, early as usual. "Does your bookstore actually make any money? You're not open a lot."

"Maxie's there again. I'm thinking about making her a partner, or just giving it to her. What is that incredible smell?"

I had finally gotten around to making raisin bread. I closed the oven door where I'd just taken out two round loaves. I slid them off the cookie sheet and onto a cooling rack. "You can afford to just give away a bookstore?"

He shrugged. "I'll give it to you for a loaf of that bread. I love homemade bread." He slammed shut the silverware drawer and turned toward me, knife in hand.

I stood in front of the counter, arms spread wide. "It has to cool. Give it ten minutes anyway."

"Five. It tastes best hot."

"Not if it all squishes up when you try to tear it apart. Besides, I thought we could take it on a picnic to the beach."

"That'll take too long. I'll die if I have to drive to Herring Cove with that smell coming from a bag in the back. I'll..." His voice trailed off as I came to stand in front of him, very close in front, and looked up to capture his gaze.

I circled my arms around his neck and tugged, bringing his face close to mine. With every word he said, everything he did, he made me feel good about myself. "I hope there's something besides my cooking that you like."

He grinned, that lopsided smile that had started my heart soaring the very first day. I just hadn't recognized it for what it was. "I can think of several things, but this is probably the foremost."

His lips were firm against mine and while I might have initiated the kiss, he quickly took over. If a person could become addicted to kisses, I was hooked. Long moments later, he slowly raised his head, gazing at me with longing in his eyes.

"Mmm, that's almost as good as homemade bread."

I punched him playfully in the stomach. "Take me to the beach and you can eat a whole loaf. I hear the sunset at Herring Cove is spectacular."

"Only when it's shared," he replied, kissing me one more time. When we finally came up for breath, he added, "Lots of things are spectacular when they're shared."

I grabbed my camera while Rob packed a bag with bottled water, a blanket and one of the loaves of bread, which had a mysterious chunk missing by the time I saw him put it in the bag.

It was hard to find a parking place at Herring Cove as the sunset in Cape Cod was one of the reasons some people visited the area. We dropped our bag on the blanket, Rob tore off another hunk of bread, and we walked down the beach toward the setting sun.

I took a few shots of wild sand roses and sea grass that lined the back of the beach. We walked along the edge of the water, holding hands and stopping now and again to share a kiss.

"Wait, I want to get a shot of Race Point with the sun setting behind it." I tugged on my hand, but he wouldn't let go. "Rob, I need both hands to balance the camera."

He actually pouted. "What if I like holding your hand?" He brought it up and kissed my fingers where they were entwined with his.

Was it any wonder I really liked this man? "You can have it back after I take a picture."

With a sigh, he released me, but when I turned to face the sun, he stepped close behind me and put his hands on my waist. I could feel his legs brush mine as he widened his stance to either side of my feet. When he settled his chin on my shoulder I started giggling.

"What are you doing?"

"I'm your tripod. I'll keep you balanced. Just do your thing and don't mind me."

Easier said than done, I thought, as his fingers wiggled along my waist and his chest touched my back. He certainly wasn't keeping me balanced in the metaphorical sense. My mind tumbled in a dozen different directions, I flushed hot, and my heart raced. All in anticipation of what he would surprise me with next.

"If you don't hurry, I'm going to have to go back for another hunk of bread." His breath tickled my ear as I tried to focus the camera.

"If you don't quit, I'll give your bread to the birds." I put the camera to my eye again.

"You wouldn't."

"Rob."

He finally stood still but when I tried to take a picture, the shutter wouldn't release. "Not again," I muttered, turning the camera off and back on.

"What's the problem?"

"I have no idea. I took pictures just minutes ago and now it won't work. It did this before, and I had to use the timer." I pushed that button, then the shutter, lifted the camera to my eye to focus and then held my breath to keep myself still. Unfortunately, Rob jiggled me right when the shutter clicked.

"You really need to find another job. You make a lousy tripod," I teased as I went through the whole process again, admonishing him to be still for thirty seconds. By this time, the sun had sunk low, and the sky was deep orange and purple. The lighthouse and keeper house stood out in dark silhouette.

"Got it," I said, turning in his arms. "Oh, look." Just beyond his shoulder was a little girl, barely walking, holding her father's hand as they walked along the very edge of the water. I automatically raised my camera and took a shot.

"Now that's really odd. This time it worked right." I frowned as I turned the camera off. "Why would it work then not work, then start working right again?"

Rob took the camera from around my neck then dragged me close. He nibbled on my lips before saying, "You want my professional opinion?"

"You can't even be a tripod, but now you're an expert?"

That earned me a lecherous grin. "Well, maybe not with cameras, but there's some other things I'm pretty good at." His gray eyes were dark as he held my gaze, intent and yet questioning, not demanding. In his gaze, I suddenly saw my future, knowing that it would be something shared, not taken; offered, not forced.

"Geez, get a room." Our mood was broken by some teenagers walking past.

"He's right. Shall we go back to your place, now that it's fixed?" Rob turned around and hand in hand, we started back to where we had left the blanket.

"I still don't have a bed, although you did say we didn't necessarily need one." I couldn't believe that popped out of my mouth, but it earned me another grin.

"Still, we'll go to my place." He handed me the bag while he shook out the blanket, tucked it under one arm and me under the other. As we walked back to the car, he whispered in my ear, "I think a bed is appropriate for your first time."

My stomach flip-flopped and I felt young and on that precipice where I knew something absolutely wonderful was about to happen. My arm snaked around his back, and I hugged him close.

"My first time. Mmm, that sounds nice."

Chapter 8
The Truth

Making love with Rob was one of the unique experiences in my life. He was a great advocate of foreplay and a very active participant. I don't think I've ever laughed so much in my life, which was a totally awesome way to go about things that otherwise could have been embarrassing. After all, while I knew the process, I hadn't been with anyone except my husband, and I hadn't even done that in a very long time.

He held me in the aftermath while I cried, whispering words that I couldn't recall but I remembered how good they made me feel. I cried for what I had been missing all those years—the intimacy of lovemaking but also the pillow talk afterwards; the cuddling and light caresses and lingering kisses. Rob rendered love-making a seven course meal where I had been living on drive-through and take-out.

Now, as I stretched and tried to get my happily weary body out of bed, I wished I had been able to skip the last unhappy years of my married life. But of course, if I hadn't gone through the bad times, I wouldn't be here now. I also wouldn't have a job I thoroughly enjoyed. And I wouldn't have met Rob. I was beginning to think he might be my reward for being a good person.

And he could cook. I followed my nose to the kitchen where bacon, an omelet, and the remains of a loaf of raisin bread were spread out on the table.

"Good morning," he said, placing a steaming cup of coffee in front of me, creamer included, as I sank into the nearest chair. He looked so great this morning, wearing khaki shorts and a tee shirt with a logo so faded I couldn't even read it. His hair was wild, as always, and a dark shadow covered his chin. Yeah, he looked really good.

He grabbed his cup and sat opposite me, digging into breakfast and passing me the platters. "I hope I didn't mess up your research by moving your papers to one end." He pointed to the stack of papers with his fork. "I didn't want to get breadcrumbs on anything."

"You left no crumbs that I can see," I said as I took the last piece of raisin bread. When he frowned, I tore it apart and gave him half, shaking my head. "All I had to do was bake you bread?" I was teasing, but I probably shouldn't have said anything. I knew we were old enough that there wouldn't be that morning after hesitation. Still, I think I needed reassurance.

"Honey, I love that you can bake bread, but it was never about that. I wanted you because of your laugh, remember?"

"I remember something about the crinkles around my eyes."

He shrugged, not the least concerned that he may have offended me. "That, too. But it goes back to your laugh. People who laugh and smile a lot have those little crinkles." He smiled to show me that he had them, too. "Besides, at our age—"

"Oh, don't even go there."

Rob was very good at taking a hint, among other things. "Okay, so tell me if you found anything interesting in that tome you were reading."

"Not really. I was trying to construct a timeline for some of the things I know. Like the lighthouses were built in 1816, but clear back in 1714 they created The Precinct of Cape Cod. Everybody was destroying the trees on the Cape, and they were afraid that too much sand would be driven into the harbor by the wind, thus making the harbor itself unserviceable."

"Fascinating," Rob said with a grimace.

I rolled my eyes. "Yeah, I know, but sometimes you have to wade through the crap to find a gem." I reached over for my papers and the notes I made. "The history is not real predictable because people appeared to abandon the area on several occasions—specifically the Revolutionary War and the Civil War." I shuffled more papers. "Oh, and look, this history says Long Point lighthouse was built in 1826 and the walking guide says 1816. It makes it kind of hard to trace the origins of things if they can't even decide when the lighthouse was built."

"What does this have to do with your cottage?"

"Nothing, I was just giving you a little history lesson." I stuck my tongue out at him. I flipped to the last page of the history I had kept. "This piece may not have to do with the cottage, but maybe it pertains to the ghost."

"The ghost that doesn't exist except in your mind?"

I sighed. "Just listen. 'The fact may be cited that not a murder has ever been committed in this town, nor has there ever been a native inhabitant of the place sentenced to state's prison.'"

"What would that have to do with a ghost?"

I loved bouncing ideas off Rob. He asked questions, making me probe deeper and he really listened to what I said, even if he didn't agree with my ideas.

"People usually linger as ghosts when they die before they accomplish what they need to do—something is left undone. Or they could still be around because of a traumatic experience."

"You just said nobody was murdered here, so it's not likely your ghost was a victim."

"But what if the murder wasn't on the land? Perhaps then, it wouldn't have been recorded in that history of Barnstable County," I countered.

"I don't understand."

"If not by land, then by..." I raised a brow in question.

"Sea," he finished, "but you're confusing your history. One if by land and two if by sea was Boston's claim to fame."

"Don't be so literal. I'm just saying that a murder or some traumatic experience could have happened at sea. We already know the ghost uses seafaring language. Perhaps we should be looking for something nautical: a ship, a captain's log...a mutiny!" I could feel my eyes widen.

My cell rang, interrupting our conversation. I almost didn't answer it as I didn't recognize the number but was happy I did. After a few minutes of conversation, I hung up and turned to Rob.

"I have a job. A large corporation in Chicago has just endowed a foundation and they want me to write the grant guidelines. They've heard of my work, and figured a person who writes grants would be a good person to construct a request for proposals that others would use."

He frowned. "Do you have to go there?"

"For a few days, to sign contracts and visit and make sure I understand the corporation's mission, philosophy, etcetera. To tell the truth, I've been so wrapped up in finding out about the cottage," I paused, feeling my face warm, "and in you, that I've forgotten about actually working for a living."

"You don't need to, you know. You could just move in with me and bake bread all day."

I laughed. "Are you ever going to get over that?" He shook his head.

"How about if I bake another batch before I leave for Chicago?"

He shook his head again. "I can live without the bread...for a few days. But I can't live without you." He came around the table and scooted my chair out. When I stood, he hugged me close. "How about if I show you what you'll be missing while you're gone?"

* * *

Getting out of Provincetown wasn't the easiest thing to do. Rob didn't want me to drive all the way to Providence, so we took the ferry to Boston, and I caught a flight from there. I had tried to talk him out of going to Boston with me, but he said he had things he could do there. He promised to meet me Thursday night when I returned, and I promised to call if there were any delays.

In the meantime, he would argue with the realtor about getting a new bed for the cottage. The cottage had come furnished, so I felt the bed should be replaced, but Henrietta said it was enough that the owners had to absorb the insurance deductible for the repairs. She would just advertise it as partially furnished when I moved out.

Rob took my phone away when I started screaming how ridiculous that was, so I also had to promise to apologize when I returned. I tossed in the caveat that I would, only if it was a really nice bed, big enough for two. He had hugged me and kissed me senseless.

I ran the battery down in my phone every day calling him. We talked about the progress I was making and about the bookstore; about the sunsets I was missing and the fact that I would be the first to commit murder in Barnstable County if I found out he was enjoying them without me. He swore he walked home every day with his eyes closed.

Being away from Rob gave me time to assess my feelings. I thought that having him around all the time was just too nice, and I wondered if getting back in the swing of my job and traveling on my own would change my feelings. It did, but not the way I feared. When I tried to sleep in a strange hotel bed, I longed for his arm around me and the warmth of his chest against my back. Even though we talked daily, I missed the touches and the way he looked at me, really interested in what I had to say.

I realized I didn't want to be alone the rest of my life and I wanted more than a casual relationship. Being able to do what I wanted when I wanted was still a rather lonely way to go through life. While I longed to have experiences and see new places, I wanted to share them with someone.

Because Rob and I started out as friends, he had seen me at my worse; he knew my darkest secrets and he had ever so gently brought me back from the brink of despair. He often put me first, and that allowed me to grow as a person. I couldn't wait to get home.

* * *

I took a cab from the Boston airport to the ferry port, just making it to the end of a long line to get my ticket when it started drizzling. I hadn't packed a jacket or an umbrella, but while I fumbled to tuck my purse under my arm to keep it dry, a large black umbrella popped up over my head. I turned to thank my benefactor and found Rob's smiling face.

I squealed, throwing my arms around him and hugging him tight, practically dislodging the umbrella.

"My gallantry will be for naught if you knock the umbrella out of my hand," he said, circling my waist with his free hand and bending for a kiss.

"I could really care less about getting wet. I'm just so glad to see you. I thought you were going to meet me at the P'town side of the ferry."

"It's best to keep you off center and constantly surprised." His grin was infectious, and I smiled in return.

148

"Hey, could you two move ahead? It's not exactly dry here." A grumpy voice from behind caused us to laugh. Apparently not everyone was happy standing in the rain.

Rob grabbed the handle of my pull bag. "Come on. I already bought your ticket." We moved to where the ferry was loading. Perhaps because of the rain, or because it was a Thursday, we didn't have long to wait before we boarded. Instead of going inside, we climbed to the second level and found a nook at the side that was protected from the rain but allowed us to be outside. Rob tucked my suitcase behind us, and then pulled me into his arms as we looked out over the harbor.

"You know by the end of the summer I'm going to have to find a place to live that has either lots of windows or a huge wrap-around deck. I don't think I can work inside anymore, away from the sunshine and sea air."

"It's not sunny today."

"You know what I mean. Being here is so open and airy. I used to be in an office with no windows. I don't think I can stand that anymore."

A spray of water came over the side and we laughed as it drenched both of us. Rob didn't comment on my thoughts about the end of summer, and I wondered if he thought I was pushing him toward a commitment. It wasn't that at all. I had little time to decide where I wanted to go at summer's end, although if I apologized nicely to Henrietta perhaps she'd let me do a month to month lease until I decided.

Along with the rain came wind and choppy seas, and we finally had to give up our hideaway for the safety of the cabin. We stumbled our way inside and collapsed on the nearest bench, content to sit and hold hands, trying not to notice all the people around us getting sick with every swell of the waves.

The drizzle had turned to rain by the time we arrived at Fisherman's Wharf. Rob offered to go get the car, but seeing as we were both already wet, I trudged along with him to the parking lot. We stopped at his house for him to grab a change of clothes and I thought we would stay there.

"There's a new bed out at your place," he said, a twinkle in his eyes. He didn't need to say any more. I hurried back to the car.

Thunder rumbled in the distance and the rain began in earnest as we drove slowly along the winding road, the windshield wipers not helping in the least. Rob missed the turn and had to back up, grumbling under his breath that this was probably a bad idea after all.

"You said you wanted to be out here the next time it stormed," I said once we were inside the house. It was quiet except for the drum of rain on the roof and the continuous thunder. "Now I suppose nothing will happen."

"And that disappoints you?" He sounded shocked. "You're kidding, right, after what happened last time?" He also sounded just a little nervous.

"If you don't believe in ghosts, you're the perfect companion for me. You'll keep me grounded and—"

Thump, thump. Heavy footsteps pounded across the floorboards above us.

"That is not some tree thunking your roof." He pulled me close to his side, his gaze on the ceiling.

Thump, thump. "Yo!"

"Yo?" he repeated.

"I told you he was a sea ghost," I whispered. I put my hand on his chest and felt his heart beating as fast as my own.

Tucking my hand in his, but keeping me behind him, Rob started down the hall. Lightning struck at that moment, casting an eerie blue glow in the hallway.

"Holy crap, did you see that?"

I was right behind him, squeezing his hand for all I was worth. It was like one of those scary Twilight Zone episodes where you knew something bad was going to happen, but you couldn't close your eyes and you couldn't look away. I lifted his arm around my shoulders and peeked around him.

"That guy—it was like he was looking right at me." He pointed to the larger than life portrait at the end of the hall. "Who the hell is that anyway?"

A shiver raced down my spine. I thought it had just been my imagination spooking me the last time, but if Rob saw it too? "Maybe it's the man who built the house?"

"He looks like a pirate guarding your door."

Thump, thump, thump. "I'll see ye all in hell!" The words were muffled by the storm, just barely distinguishable.

I clutched my arms around his waist. "I don't think he likes being called a pirate."

"It's got to be the wind. I don't believe in ghosts." He took another step toward the portrait, reaching for the doorknob.

"Wait," I said, tugging at his waist. "We don't really have to go up there. At least let's wait for the storm to blow through."

"We might as well go up while the lights are still on." He grabbed the doorknob and twisted. "It's locked." I watched as he checked around the knob for a button to turn. "How can it be locked?"

I shook my head. "I don't think it has a lock. Most inside doors don't, do they?"

Rob rattled the knob again. I could feel his muscles tighten as he tugged, but to no avail.

Another clap of thunder shook the house, the lights flickered and went out, pitching us in absolute dark.

"Do you have a flashlight?"

"No." I did, but I wasn't going to get it for him. I wasn't moving from his side, and hoped he wouldn't insist on going upstairs in the dark.

He turned around and together we shuffled back down the hall toward the living room. "I thought you wanted an adventure," he said as we lit the lanterns and settled down on the couch. "We could probably see enough with one of these."

"If you can get past the locked door. Besides, been there, done that." I shivered, recalling the last storm.

He tugged me close as he relaxed against the couch. "Well, this is rather romantic anyway. A rainy night, candlelight, and a warm, soft woman at my side." He kissed the top of my head. "A warm soft woman in a warm soft bed would be better, but I think we can make do."

"You're not afraid of what's up there?"

I felt his chin scrape against my head as he shook it. "No.

There's a logical explanation for the noise."

"What about what he said?"

"I didn't hear anything except the thumping." He kissed my temple then trailed his lips down my cheek.

I pushed against his chest, levering myself to see if he was teasing, but I couldn't read his expression in the weak glow from the lanterns. "You're kidding. You didn't hear him swear at us?"

Rob shook his head, tucking me back down beside him as he turned and stretched out full length on the couch. Maybe I had imagined it. Given how badly the last storm frightened me, I might well be projecting that onto tonight. Yet I knew I hadn't dreamed what happened last time. Whoever—whatever—was upstairs during the storm had saved my life. Now tonight, extremely happy to be on this side of the locked door, and with Rob, I only hoped the spirit still felt benevolent and meant us no harm.

Chapter 9
The Cupola

The thing about being "middle-aged" is that while making love is nice, it isn't the be-all-end-all of our relationship. We were content to cuddle on the couch in the dark and talk.

"I forgot to tell you, after I came out when your bed was delivered—a bed it doesn't look like we'll use," Rob added with sarcasm, "I took your camera into the shop and had it looked at. There's nothing wrong with it."

"I hadn't used it since; I forgot about the glitch. I wonder what caused it?" I turned to him. "You are wonderful, you know that?" He didn't make a facetious remark or tease me. He stared solemnly back at me, and I wondered what he was thinking. "Thank you," I added. It was a small gesture, seeing about my camera, but I wanted him to know I appreciated him.

He leaned forward and kissed me on the nose. I'd found he did that whenever he wanted to kiss me but didn't want to get into the really heavy stuff. And I liked it. I kissed his nose right back.

"I wonder why it didn't like taking pictures of the Race Point lighthouse," I mused. More thunder rumbled in the distance, the storm angling its way past us. "I should try taking a picture of our ghost." I held my breath and listened but heard no rumblings from above. Perhaps the excitement for the evening had passed. Even so, I wasn't sure I wanted to venture upstairs. "Too bad the door's locked," I added for good measure. Since Rob said he didn't believe in ghosts, it would be just like him to try to break the door down.

"I've got a toolbox in the jeep, but there's not enough light to do anything tonight." He wiggled around to get more comfortable. "We might as well just settle down here."

I scooted down a little, putting my head on his stomach. "I like it fine here. You make a good pillow."

He snorted. "And here I've been exercising while you were gone to get ripped."

I patted his stomach. "I don't think I want you ripped. I like you just the way you are."

His hand caressed my shoulder. "I like you very much the way you are, too." Rob wrapped his other arm around me, and I soon heard the soft even rhythm of his breathing in sleep. I closed my eyes, a sense of contentment stealing over me that I hadn't felt in a very long time.

"Hey." Rob wiggled my shoulders, "I have to get up."

I groaned, lifting my weight enough for him to slide out from under me, but when I flopped back onto the couch it wasn't nearly as comfortable. I heard him flip a switch and the hall light came on.

"At least the storm passed without any damage this time," he mumbled on the way to the bathroom.

"We haven't been upstairs yet," I reminded him, sitting up and rubbing my face. I still felt tired, even though I knew I had slept like a rock last night. Somewhere in my subconscious there must have still been stress from the storm.

"Well, I'll be damned."

I turned to glance down the hall where Rob stood, the door to the loft wide open. Regardless of my achy bones, I jumped up, hurrying over to stand beside him. Well, actually, I stayed a little behind him.

"How'd you get it unlocked?"

"It wasn't locked. I just turned the knob and it opened."

I looked at him. "That's spooky."

He shrugged his shoulders as if indifferent, but his puzzled expression said otherwise. "It must swell with the amount of moisture in the air. That's why it stuck." He pushed the door forward and back, opened it, closed it then opened it again, but there didn't seem to be any part of it that stuck now. He swung it closed again, frowning.

"Why don't you put the coffee on while I get my toolbox? I'm still going to take down this ugly picture." He stood with hands on hips looking at the portrait, the larger than life man staring back at us with the same stance.

"I don't know," I said, walking back down the hall, "I've kind of gotten used to him being there." I thought about the locked door last night. "Maybe he's guarding my virtue."

A surprised squawk erupted from me as Rob caught me from behind.

"You don't need a pirate guarding you from me."

I laughed as he picked me up and spun in a circle, finally pinning me against the wall. Our gazes met and I held my breath. His kiss was as gentle as a spring rain, but the promise of so much more was in his touch as he cupped my face.

He broke the kiss but continued to stand close, his legs bracketing mine as I leaned against the wall. This man had become so dear to me in such a short amount of time. What was going to happen at the end of the summer?

"I only have a month to get the basic grant requirements written for the Imaging.com Corporation, and I have a month left on the rental on the cottage," I whispered, almost choking as I tried to get the words out. "I don't want you to think I'm avoiding you, but I'm going to have to put in a lot of hours. I do have to work for a living."

He didn't move, didn't pull away, but just kept staring at me with those soulful gray eyes. Then he slowly shook his head. "You don't have to work, Bonnie, not if you don't want to. You must know I want to take care of you; I would—"

I put my hand over his mouth. Even though I had thought about it on the boat, I didn't want to hear him proclaim himself when I was just beginning to take those steps in our relationship. However, I did need him to know how important he was to me.

"Rob, it's something I have to do for now. It's part of who I am. You have become someone very important to me, but I can't come to you a broken, hollow person with no depth; no sense of self or feelings that what I do makes a difference. Your caring and gentle patience have helped me gain back my self-esteem and sense of worth, but I doubt I'm done developing."

"You feel pretty well developed to me," he teased, but in his gaze I saw respect and caring, and I knew how very lucky I was to have found him. "You've made incredible progress this summer, BJ, but I hope you realize that all of us humans are in a continual state of change. If we're lucky, that part of us never stops."

"I know. I just need to be sure of who I am before I can give myself away again."

"Does that mean I can't see you at all?" He had the most delightful pout, which he tended to use on me quite a bit. While I saw through it, I was happy to indulge him in this regard.

"I'm not working right now."

* * *

Rob lay sideways in my huge, very soft, new bed, staring at the ceiling, his head turning back and forth as he followed the roof line. His hand casually caressed my shoulder, but I don't think he even realized it. I finally propped my chin on my hands, which were splayed on his chest, and settled my gaze on his face. The years had been good to him, and whatever life had thrown at him didn't register in lines and wrinkles. We never really talked about age, and now I wondered if I was sleeping with a younger man.

After the christening we had just given my new bed, whatever age difference there might be apparently didn't bother Rob.

"What are you thinking?" I asked, my voice sounding loud in the silence of the late morning.

"Hmm? Just wondering why there's no trap door to that cupola."

I pushed against his chest, levering myself up so I could see his eyes. As I suspected, they were twinkling with

160

mischief. I decided to play the outraged victim anyway.

"I just..." I could feel my face heat at the thought of what I had just done with him. I couldn't say it out loud. "After what we just did, you're thinking about the damned cupola?"

He grinned. "I have to think of something besides you or I'll never recover." He pulled me back into his arms. "You turn me inside out and upside-down. I think about you all the time. If I'm with you, I want to do things that please you. When I'm away from you, I count the hours until I can see you again."

By the time he was done, hot tears streamed down my cheeks, and I bit my lip to keep it from trembling. "That's so sweet," I blubbered.

"Guys aren't sweet." He dabbed at my eyes with the sheet. "We're macho, gruff, and like to hunt and fish and play with tools." He rolled me over, gave me a quick kiss and scooted off the bed. "Speaking of which, you sidetracked me and I never did get my toolbox...or my coffee."

"I don't know what you expect to find, but since you insist on getting up, I guess there's no hope for it." I quickly grabbed some clothes and hurried toward the stairs. "Dibs on the bathroom."

By the time I took a quick shower and dressed, I could smell coffee brewing but there was no sign of Rob in the house. I fixed two cups and wandered out the front door to find him standing in the small sand yard staring at the roof.

"What's wrong?" I handed him a cup of coffee.

"Nothing. I can't find a ladder to get up on the roof, but now that I really look at that thing, it doesn't much look like a cupola. Don't those things have little pointed caps or something?"

I looked up. The cupola had wooden slats running vertically around it, almost like a barrel. "Maybe it's a flat roofed cupola?"

Rob glanced from the structure, along the line of the roof then back. "Something else is funny. Your bedroom is in a loft, but I don't think it's as long as the house. What else is at either end—a closet, storage?"

I shook my head. "The closet is along one side, not an end. It's not real big and the ceiling of it slopes to match the roof."

"Hmm." Rob handed his empty mug back to me and headed inside, pulling his tape measure from his belt as he went. I quickly followed, not wanting to be left behind on whatever adventure he had in mind. I was just happy he ignored the portrait on the door as he swung it open and took the stairs two at a time.

"Hold this right here." He motioned to the end of the tape measure and when I took it, he walked to the other end of the loft, measuring the basic length of the house.

"Let go." When I did, the tape zapped back into the reel. I had to hurry to keep up with him as he bounded back down the stairs and outside.

"Rob, for Pete's sake. What are you doing?"

He didn't comment as he handed me the end of the tape again at one corner of the house, then paced to the opposite end. "Aha! The house is ten feet longer than what your loft space measures."

"And this means...what?"

He grabbed my hand, and we once again went in and up the stairs. I think I would have measured the outside of the house first to save a trip, but I wasn't about to tell him that, him being a tool guy and all.

When we got upstairs, he started banging on the wall along the end by the stairs. "The cupola is at this end of the house, but not over your loft. That's why we can't see a trap door leading to it from here."

"Maybe it's just for looks and doesn't have a—" My sentence was cut short when, under Rob's pounding, a hidden spring-loaded door opened, its edge running perfectly along a groove in the light colored paneling.

"Oh, yeah," Rob grinned. "You can have your ghost. I'll take secret doors and passageways any day."

It was too dark to see far into the space but I had no desire to venture there. Cobwebs hung across the entrance, some that had been attached to the door now drifting down onto the floor. A chill draft crept along the floor, sweeping past me and raising goose bumps on my legs. Rob pulled a flashlight from the hip pocket of his jeans, pointing the beam of light into the dark cavern. He reached for my hand, but I held back.

"I don't think I want to go in there." A shiver ran down my back and I swore I heard moaning coming from within.

Rob poked his head past the door, brushing cobwebs out of the way as he went. "Sweetie, there doesn't look to be anything in here except for an old trunk or two and lots and lots of cobwebs." I could hear the humor in his voice and punched him playfully in the back.

"Cobwebs are spooky. Don't spiders make cobwebs? And with that many cobwebs, there has to be lots and lots of spiders."

He turned and looked at me. "Spiders make spider webs. Besides, your ghost might be in here."

"That's just what I needed to know!" I practically shouted, not understanding why I was so frightened of what appeared to be just unused storage space. "I was much happier thinking he was outside somewhere."

Rob could see I was frightened, and he stepped away from the opening. "Go downstairs and get a broom and I'll get rid of all the cobwebs before you go in." He raised a brow to see if that would appease me.

I knew I was being foolish. Rob wouldn't let anything happen to me. "Will you knock out the wall and put in a window before I get back?" I heard him laugh as I trudged down the stairs.

I returned a few minutes later, but Rob was nowhere in sight.

"Rob?" I hadn't heard a crash or any thumping, but a grown man just didn't disappear.

"Rob?" I started to panic. The arctic air drifting through the open secret door made me think of all kinds of scary crap happening.

"Rob!" This time I heard thumping and I screamed.

"Yikes, baby. Hold on." Rob grabbed my arms and shook me.

My eyes popped open, taking in the cobwebs that clung to his hair and shirt. He was safe. I punched him in the arm.

"Do not ever...ever scare me like that again! I didn't know where you were. I thought something had gotten you."

"Because you weren't here to protect me?" He had the audacity to grin. I punched him again.

"Hey, okay. I'm sorry, but I was on the roof, and I didn't hear you until you started screaming. Then I about broke my neck getting back down the ladder."

I narrowed my gaze. "You were on the roof? What ladder?"

"You have to see this. I found a trap door in the ceiling, and it leads to your cupola." He grabbed my hand, but I held back. "There's nothing in here," he promised.

"What was the thumping?"

"Probably just me walking around up there to make sure it was safe."

My curiosity got the better of me, and besides, it had to be warmer outside on the roof than standing in the arctic draft. I clutched Rob's hand with both of mine as he led me into the shadowy gloom of the sealed off attic. The flashlight made it scarier than being in the dark when Rob kept bouncing it off the walls and floor. But right in the center of the gloom, light shone down from the roof where he had left the trap door open.

He stopped by a ladder poking up through the opening.

"Go ahead, climb up."

"Where'd the ladder come from?"

"It's actually hinged to the ceiling." He pointed with the flashlight. "I was busy looking around on the floor and almost missed it. When I grabbed the end rung and pulled, the ladder swung down and revealed the trap door. It's even circular," he continued, and it took me a second to realize he meant the trap door, not the ladder.

"Hold on to the rungs of the ladder when you climb," he instructed. "I'll be right behind you. There's not a lot of room up there and the hole is right in the middle, so when you get to the top, move to the side so I can get through."

Climbing the ladder made me nervous, but the minute I stepped onto the narrow platform, I forgot all about how I got there. A spectacular view of trees arched around me like a leafy green canopy, the ground a brilliant display of red and pink roses, blue and white hydrangeas. Off to my left the ocean, crystal blue, reflected the sun. I could see just a scrap of beach beyond the trees. I lifted my head and inhaled, catching the sea breeze and salt-tinged air.

"Scoot." Rob prodded me in the backside, reminding me to move. No more than five feet in diameter, the entire cupola barely had room for the two of us to stand on the platform. When Rob stepped off the last rung of the ladder, he straddled the opening and leaned back against the railing.

"Is that safe?"

"I checked it out," he said. "The cupola straddles the peak of the roof, and it looks like notches were cut at the bottom, front and back, to make it fit secure before they nailed it down. The platform came afterwards, I think, to have a level surface to stand on."

"It's round," I commented, as I slid my hand along the curved surface of the railing that topped the structure. "You would think it would have been easier, given the pitch of the roof, to build something square." Wood slats were topped off with the railing and the whole thing was about waist high on Rob. "It's like standing in a rain barrel, but up high," I said with a grin.

I looked around again, enjoying the feeling of being above the ground and it reminded me of my cousin's tree house back when we were young. I could discern the back end of Rob's jeep just past the roof. "We could spy on people from up here," I said. "If anyone ever came out. This is really cool, but I wonder why they didn't put a cover on it. With all the rain we've been having, how come it isn't full of water?"

"There are small drainage holes along the sides, so any water flows out and onto the roof. Besides, there are gaps between the slats. I can't tell for sure without leveling it, but it feels there's just the slightest slope to the platform, so that would keep it from seeping through the trap door."

I turned and looked at him. "You just have this all figured out, don't you?"

He leaned forward, hands on the rail to either side of me, getting right in my face. "I think I've found a place where you can't run and hide from me." He bent to lightly kiss me.

I guess in some ways, I was still hiding, even when I was right there. But it was getting better. Keeping my heels backed up against the wood slats so I wouldn't accidentally step into the trap door hole, I circled his neck and returned his kiss, putting some heat into my response. I felt the cords of his neck muscles tighten but he didn't touch me with anything other than his lips.

"Damn, that's not fair at all," he groused when I finally let him come up for air.

"What's not?"

"I worried about flipping us both right over the railing if I didn't hold onto it, so I couldn't hold on to you..." His voice faded and he got a strange look on his face. I could feel him slide his left hand back and forth, looking past my shoulder to the railing.

"Hey, you know what? I don't think this cupola was built onto this house. I think it was already created for another reason and placed here when the house was built."

"I don't believe you. I poured my heart and soul into that kiss!"

He grinned. "I know, and I fully intend to get back to you on that, but as long as we're up here, turn around slowly and look."

I shuffled my feet and turned within the confines of his arms. He pointed to a place on the railing where a small circular indentation still scarred the wood.

"I do believe, my dear, that you have an original crow's nest here. It's the right shape, size, and that little hatch in the bottom would have been open so the sailor could slide down the main mast to the yard in order to crawl down the rigging. That would also explain why it isn't enclosed. A crow's nest was used for observation." He pointed to the indentation. "This is where they embedded the compass."

"How do you know a compass was there?" I slid my hand along the indention.

"I do read some of the books I buy, you know. The crow's nest always had a compass, even though the captain had more sophisticated nautical instruments."

"So, what does that mean?"

"The compass would have been on the forward side of the crow's nest; the side facing the bow." He looked around and down as though trying to orient himself with the rest of the house. "If this house were a ship and we're facing the bow, this would be larboard or port," he put out his left arm, "and that would be starboard." He put out his right arm. "Didn't you say he yelled at you to go to starboard?"

"He? I thought you didn't believe in ghosts."

"Hey, I'm trying to help you out here. Isn't it a requirement or something for a reader to suspend his disbelief in order to really get into the story? Besides, maybe you'll make a believer out of me."

"You are so full of it," I told him, "but yes, that's what he said."

"So going to the right from your bed would...take you to the stairs and away from where the tree limb came in. Come on." He carefully climbed down the short stairs, stopping part way until I had gotten my footing on the ladder. Once down, he quickly climbed far enough to close the trap door.

I didn't look anywhere except at his rear end as I waited. I wasn't ready to see what might be lurking in the dark corners now that he had closed off the only source of light.

As soon as he swung the ladder back into place, I grabbed his hand and hurried out of the storage space, making him close the secret door behind us.

He looked around my bedroom. "If you'd gone larboard or left instead of right, you would have been trapped in the corner there." He pointed to the small space between the bed and a dresser. "Wow, maybe there is something to this after all."

"At least now I have something to go on to identify him. All this only confirms that the ghost might have been a sailor, like I mentioned after reading all that history about no murders being committed on land. He's apparently haunting a crow's nest and uses nautical language."

"Well, that certainly narrows it down." Rob sounded a bit sarcastic. "Do you know how many people here are descendants of sailors and seafaring people?"

"All of them?"

He rolled his eyes. "Just about."

Chapter 10
Discovering the Truth

Now that Rob had started to believe there may be something mysterious going on at the cottage—he wasn't ready to say there was an actual ghost—he came out every day. One day he even showed up with a collapsible spyglass he found at an antique store. He'd wait until close to supper time, respecting my need to get a day's work completed. I teased him about only coming out so he could climb into the cupola and wait for the ghost, not to see me.

He would swear adamantly that wasn't the case, then ruin his defense by asking if I'd heard in the evening's forecast that it might rain. Like a little boy on a new adventure, there was no hope for him. While I wouldn't venture into that dark, secret area of the loft, I happily let him play because he often stayed the night, even if it didn't rain.

He'd either bring dinner with him or he'd cook out on the deck. I could become very used to him taking care of me and worried constantly about what would happen at the end of the summer. One night I decided to ask, sort of.

"What happens after tourist season?"

"To Provincetown? Or to us?" He saw through my ruse.

I took a sip of my wine to gather my courage to ask what I really wanted to know. As had been the case most of the summer, Rob rescued me once again.

"Provincetown becomes this quiet, slow-paced burg. Many of the shops and B&B's shut down. It's the perfect place for a writer—all open spaces; quiet with nobody to bother you." He turned from watching the sunset to capture my gaze. "Well, almost nobody, and there's a great bookstore that stays open year-round for access to some terrific research books."

His serious demeanor lightened. "I could be your research assistant. I could wear a white lab coat."

I smiled. "Writers don't wear lab coats."

"Maybe a tee shirt then, that says Assistant to Well-known, Famous Author."

That made me laugh. "You are very good for my ego, even though I believe well-known and famous may be synonyms. Speaking of research, I've been trying to find out more about the cottage and cupola and who might have built it."

Rob shook his head. "I don't know about the cottage, but I believe the cupola was put up there as an intact crow's nest. So, you need to be researching ships." He started to say something more, snapped his mouth shut and glared at me. "What?"

"I've been staying away all day thinking you were working on your Imaging.com account and you've been out cruising the net?"

"I'm almost finished with the rough draft of the RFP. It'll have to be looked over by their legal team, and then I'll have to set up a test group. But whenever I need a little break from all the highbrow jargon, I get online and look stuff up. The problem is there's nothing to go on. I need a name, like for that guy whose portrait is on the door. I've traced records on the cottage but can't find out who built it."

"You've looked up records on this house?"

Whoops. And then I realized that I wanted him to know my plans. "I was thinking about the possibility of buying the cottage."

"Nice thought processes." He gave a nod and a smile.

"But I wanted to deal directly with the owners instead of that old biddy at the realty office."

"And?" He could easily read me and knew I wasn't happy.

"And guess who actually owns the cottage?"

He looked at me with a brow raised. When I continued to frown, he laughed out loud. "Why did Henrietta make such a big deal out of renting it to you if she owns it? You'd think she would be happy making some money off it." He gave a dramatic sigh before adding, "Maybe you'll have to let me use my charm and make a deal for you."

"Someone will have to because I don't think I've made any points with her." I picked up our glasses and headed back into the kitchen.

"BJ, what did you do?"

"Nothing," I called over my shoulder. I hadn't really, as long as thoughts didn't count as action.

Rob followed me back into the house and helped clean up the kitchen from our dinner. "Let's take a walk," he suggested as he hung up the dish cloth.

"On the beach?" I loved walking along the edge of the water, feeling the sand beneath my feet while the cool waves lapped my legs.

"Of course," he replied, kissing my nose. "There's supposed to be a full moon tonight, but it won't be up for awhile."

"Oh, so taking a walk with me is just a time killer until you can go back up into the cupola with your telescope and look at the moon?"

He herded me toward the door. "It's a spyglass and there are lots better things to do while waiting for the moon to rise, believe me. That's why I have to get you out of the house."

I glanced back over my shoulder to see him frowning. I stopped to slip on my Crocs to walk down the path. "Rob, what's the problem?"

He sighed and ran a hand down his face. "Since I met you, all I want to do is take you to bed and love you. All day and all night. I've never had that problem before, even when I was a much younger man."

I smiled. "That's not exactly what I would call a problem."

"The word is obsession, Bonnie. I'm obsessed with you, even though I know you need time to figure out what you want. I know this job is important to you, too, but some days it drives me nuts wanting to be with you." He had taken one step down the deck stairs and turned back to me, putting us at eye level.

I looped my arms around his shoulders. I wanted so much to tell him how I felt, but previous hurts kept me mute. He stood there, patiently waiting for me to say something.

"I have so much history," I blurted out.

"Hell, honey, everyone our age has history. That's what makes us the loveable characters we all are. But it's more important to think about the present, or the history you want to make in the future."

"I told you I was thinking about buying the cottage," I said softly. "You have to figure that means I'm also thinking about staying around."

He finally gave me a reluctant smile. "And believe me that's the best news I've had in a long time." He swatted me on the behind and together we walked down the path to the beach.

* * *

Working as a freelance writer was the best job in the world, but at times I tended to work too much. Easy to get wrapped up in a project, I didn't always take enough time off for myself. I didn't want to do that with Rob, so I promised myself that I wouldn't work on weekends, but since that was his busy time at the store, I adjusted my schedule to take my days off on Monday and Tuesday. We spent our time exploring the Cape, or at least I did since Rob was a resident. He knew all the neat little hole-in-the-wall restaurants with the best seafood, took me on a tour of the Truro wine vineyard, and we even managed to squeeze in a trip to Nantucket.

It didn't make any difference if we went somewhere or just spent time at the beach collecting sea glass and unique rocks, watching the tide come in. We talked about everything, argued about a lot when it came to things dear to our hearts: women's rights for me; the environment and endangered species for Rob. But our arguments were more in the form of good-natured debates, and I found myself changing my mind on some things simply because I hadn't had correct information or hadn't really thought about it before. After all, being from a land-locked state, I didn't often think about whales and dolphins and the endangered coral reefs.

"Wake up, sleepyhead." Rob prodded me as he jumped out of bed.

I opened one eye to find the room dark. "What's wrong?"

"Nothing. I'm taking you fishing." I heard him shuffle around the room. "Watch your eyes."

"Augh!" The light on the dresser flared. "It's dark outside. Fish can't see worms in the dark." I snuggled back under the sheet.

"It'll be dawn by the time we get you a license and get down to the beach. Come on, you're burning daylight."

Rob was forever quoting movie lines. "We're not going on a cattle drive, and you're not John Wayne."

"Same principle." He came to the side of the bed, dropping my tee shirt and sweats on top of me. "I promise you a vanilla latte."

Well, there you had it. I could be bribed with coffee, and he knew my favorite.

Half an hour later we were on the beach, lawn chairs in place and Rob was threading line through my brand new pink fishing pole with flashing lights. I have no idea where he found such a thing, but he gifted me with it when we got out of the Jeep.

"This is guaranteed to catch fish, right?" I asked.

He mumbled something I didn't understand. It's hard to understand a man who had fishing line between his teeth as he tightened the intricate knot for the lure.

The sky was lightening, and the wispy clouds just above the horizon turned pink. It was totally amazing that if you stood really still and watched, you could actually see the sun rise in the sky, one inch at a time, until it was bright enough you couldn't look right at it anymore. The crisp air made me glad to have a sweatshirt. I learned that it was best to dress in layers as I never knew if the day would turn warm or remain cool.

"Do you know how to cast?" Rob asked as he handed me the pole and started assembling his gear.

"Of course. I have been fishing before." I didn't add that it was more than twenty years ago.

Thirty minutes later, after getting my line totally tangled, then the lure snagged offshore, Rob was giving me the evil eye. He had to wade out in the water, sweats tugged up his thighs, because I had worn flip-flops which he informed me were not fishing shoes.

"I thought we were fishing from the shore."

He threw up his hands. "Do you want to go back?"

I knew how much he enjoyed fishing, and the day promised to be sunny and warm. "No. How about if you fish and I watch?"

The middle of August brought the height of tourist season, so Rob actually had to work. I really pushed to get my own projects completed. I created a test RFP for Imaging.com and sent it out to a select group of organizations I worked with before. They would complete the 'Request For Proposals' for a project they had in mind, along with completing an evaluation on the actual RFP, and they would all receive a small grant from Imaging.com for their help. Although I felt the proposal was complete, sometimes I read right over the simplest of errors.

I drove into town and made a brief stop at the Maritime Museum, but no one could help me and I wasn't sure how to go about finding what I needed. How do you find the name of a ship when you have the crow's nest, but nothing else? I did find a long, long list of ships that had been wrecked, lost, or otherwise abandoned, all registered to Provincetown Port, so I requested a copy of that to at least show I had accomplished something that day. I planned to go over to the Pokey Reader and help Rob, so I might use his internet connection to look up some of the names.

I knew Rob had a couple of parking places behind the store, so I pulled into one and entered the store from the back. I walked around the corner by his office and heard voices, so I poked my head in the door.

Before I could say anything, my heart started pounding and my life shattered on the floor in a million pieces. Rob stood by his desk, his arms wrapped around a willowy brunette, his cheek on her head. He must have heard me gasp, because his head came up and he stared at me.

He didn't say a word, and for all of thirty seconds, I wanted to scream and rant at him. If ever there were a black moment in the book of my life, this was it. Well, this was the second one, and I thought I had learned from the first. We continued to stare at each other, and I realized it wasn't guilt or betrayal I saw in his gaze, but trust and love. He was asking if I trusted him?

I took a deep breath, held it as I glanced away then back. Yes, I did trust him, with my heart and my love. He knew my history and he wasn't the kind of guy to betray me. Whatever was going on, he would explain without me having to ask.

When my brain quit barraging me with questions that I now knew didn't need answers, I realized the woman in his arms was crying.

"Excuse me; I'll come back later," I said softly.

I hadn't realized how the whole situation must have looked from Rob's point of view, because when I spoke without anger, I saw him visibly relax, and smile at me. He winked and blew me a kiss and I felt a whole lot better than if I had thrown a tantrum. Besides, there was no need.

"Sweetie, think you can pull it together to meet someone?" He bent his head and spoke to the young woman, who sniffled then turned around to look at me. Rob put his arm around her shoulders, and I told myself again that I trusted him. I really did.

"Bonnie, this is my daughter, Faith. Sweetpea, Bonnie is a super good friend of mine."

His daughter gave me a watery smile. "Hi. I'm really sorry to be here bothering Dad, but I didn't get into medical school this term, and I really thought I would."

"I'm sorry to hear that," I commented, not knowing what else to say. We talked about our families and kids often, and I thought his daughter was only in college.

"It's not like she's supposed to be in med school," Rob said. "She went through college in two years, and Boston University School of Medicine would prefer she be a bit older before she starts."

"It's still not fair," Faith pouted. "If I have the prerequisites, I should get in."

"It helps to have the maturity to go with it. Dougie Houser, M.D. was only a television show. That doesn't happen in real life."

I heard a bell ring, and Rob looked toward the front of the store.

"I'll handle it," I said, but he was quick to jump in.

"No, I'll get it." As he walked by me, he whispered, "Would you take her shopping or something? I have never been good at handling her tears."

I shook my head and smiled. Endearing quality number...what...one hundred? Rob was a softy for tears.

"Come on, Faith, we're going shopping, on your dad," I added in a loud voice to be sure Rob would hear.

We went in and out of practically every store on Commercial Street, buying a few things but mostly just visiting like a couple of old friends. Faith thought her dad was beyond wonderful and kept hinting that he would make someone a good husband. Her mom had been gone a long time and she knew her dad was lonely. Actually, she didn't hint but came right out and asked.

"So, you and Dad have a thing going?" We were sitting in the Purple Feather dessert shop. She stirred her iced tea with her straw, studiously avoiding my gaze.

I waited until she looked up, then I smiled and said, "Yeah, we do. Is that okay with you?"

"Is it a really hot thing? I think he needs something really exciting in his life."

I almost choked. I wasn't used to my own kids being this straightforward. "I think that's best kept between your dad and me."

She grinned and nodded. "I like you. I think you'll be good for him." She sobered.

"But if you hurt him, I will personally come and tear your heart out."

Her cell rang, saving me from having to come up with a response. "Yeah, okay. We're about done here anyway." She hung up. "Dad says he'll buy us dinner before I take the ferry back to Boston if we get over there right now. I think he's afraid if we stay gone too long, I'll max out his credit card."

* * *

After dinner, I said goodbye to Faith and drove back to the cottage. I wanted to give Rob time alone with his daughter. He tried to talk her into staying a couple of days, but she winked at me and said she had things to do. I liked her. A lot like Rob she seemed a very happy and loving person.

I had begun researching the list of ship names from the museum when Rob came by later that night. He kissed me on the neck as he went by on his way to the cupola. Talk about obsessed. I began to wonder if he hadn't swapped one obsession for another. But he stopped at the picture door, gave a sigh, and turned back.

I hid a smile as I studiously bent over my work. In seconds, I felt hot lips on my neck and one kiss led to another until we were on the couch and into some really heavy petting. From there it quickly escalated into the hot stuff Faith wanted for her dad, and I was

184

more than happy to oblige, although I wouldn't dream of telling her I had.

"Come up to the heavens with me," he whispered as he scooted us around so we could lie side by side. "I will show you the stars and the moon and spout poetry if you want."

"Have you been reading in the romance section again?"

"Not unless it has your name on the cover."

"You really need to broaden your horizons," I replied although secretly pleased that he found my books interesting.

"I'm having a good time right where I'm at. And I do mean that literally," he said, bending low to kiss me. "Oh, if I were only in my twenties again. I could keep going all night."

I laughed. "You'd have to wish for me to be there too, or I wouldn't be able to keep up with you."

"You're right. Besides, my daughter is in her twenties, and I never want to go through that angst again. Ever."

"Speaking of, she's an absolute delight."

"She has a lot of her mother in her," he said, but without sadness.

"If you'd heard her this afternoon, I doubt you would say that. She's just like you." I pushed against him and got up from the couch.

By the time I came out of the bathroom, Rob had disappeared, so I put on a pot of coffee and sat back down at the computer. I was getting nowhere with my research, and as soon as the coffee was done, I would take some up the stairs to Rob. I would only venture into the hole, as I had come to call it, if he was already there, and if there was light.

Thump, thump, thump.

Rob must be coming down from the cupola, and now would probably drag me away from work to go look at the stars. I smiled. That was okay, because I enjoyed spending as much time with him as I could, but if I really wanted to work, he respected that and stayed out of my way.

Thump, thump. The sound was getting closer when suddenly the lights flickered off and on then off again. "Yo!"

I screamed, jumping up from the desk and racing down the hall to run smack into a large body. I opened my mouth to scream again when the lights came back on and Rob stood there, a huge grin on his face, hand on the light switch.

"That is so not funny," I yelled.

He started laughing. "I'm sorry. I just couldn't resist." He curled an arm around me and tried to hug me close, but I fought him. My heart was still racing even as I told myself I had nothing to fear. It was just Rob playing a joke.

I leaned back in his embrace and gave him the evil eye, which only made him laugh harder. He bent down to kiss my nose, but I backed off.

"Will you forgive me if I tell you what I found upstairs?"

"It depends. Cobwebs and spiders don't count."

"How about secret compartments and journals?"

Chapter 11
Finding the Answer

I gasped. "You'd better not be joking about that." I stepped back and he let me go, bringing his hands to his chest, holding what looked like a very old ledger of some sort. I made a grab for it and he raised it above his head.

"For the price of a kiss."

I narrowed my gaze. I would give him what he wanted—more than he wanted. I cupped his cheeks, slanting my lips across his, putting a lot of heat into the kiss. It took about fifteen seconds for his arms to drop, and I heard the book thud on the floor. Just about the time his arms came around me, I released him, pushing against his chest to throw him off balance.

While he stumbled against the wall, I spun around, scooped up the book and took off for the kitchen.

"You didn't have to get brutal. I would have given it to you," he pouted as he followed me.

I was already sitting at the table, gazing at the book. I looked up at him.

"What?" he asked.

"I want so badly for this to be something worthwhile." I sighed. "What if it's nothing?"

"Well, you won't know if you don't open it." He sat down beside me and reached for it. "Here, I found it; I'll do it."

I slapped at his hand. "We'll do it."

My hand shook as I carefully lifted the front cover of the ledger then my heart dropped when I saw it was blank. "Damn, damn, damn," I whispered.

Rob was looking over my shoulder and reached for the edge of the page. "Get a grip; maybe it wasn't started right at the beginning."

When he turned the page, spidery writing filled the next, almost too faded to read. I tilted the book toward the light. The date at the top said, '19 October 1890'. I looked up, smiled, and kissed Rob quick and hard. "You found a treasure!"

"More than one this summer, it would seem," he replied.

I gently nudged him with my shoulder to let him know I heard, but my real attention was on the book.

"Listen to this. *'I be Isaac Shoemaker, first mate to Captain Seamus Aberdeen of the ship Adelpha. I be lucky to survive the mutiny, being the Captain's first mate and loyal to him, and even luckier to wash ashore at Race Point after the shipwreck. When I come to my senses weeks ago, I walked the shoreline but ain't nothing left of the Adelpha 'cept the crow's nest. No crew—*

all dead, I 'magine, or scattered inland to seek their fortune naught to do with seafaring vessels. Not after what happened aboard the Adelpha.'"

I know my eyes were round as saucers when I looked up. "I am totally freaked out! This is history. And we're living in it and reading about it."

Rob looked confused. "It's not like the first time you've read a history book."

"But this is a primary source, written by a person who was living it. A diary or a journal is so much more authentic." I turned the page of the journal. "This page is dated in March, 1900, ten years later." I looked up, disappointed. "Dang, what happened in-between? This certainly isn't a day by day diary, is it?" I looked down at the writing.

"'I got little time left; the consumption taking me air and strength. Gets so as I cain't sleep for fits of coughing, so might as well get finished with what I got to do. Me Maude will have a place to stay the rest of her life. Wanted her to move down Virginia way to her sister's, but she insists she's a fisherman's wife and a fisherman's wife she'll die. Don't seem to make no never mind to her that I don't fish no more.

"'Got some buddies to set the old crow's nest atop the roof and faced it north to Race Point, where the old captain drawed his last breath. The words he yelled when we was standing aboard his ship still make me shiver. I jest hope the good captain knows I

had naught to do with the crew's mutiny. "I'll haunt ye all till every last one of ye's dead and in hell," he yelled afore they pushed him overboard. Some days I'm thinking he did just that, for it was at almost the exact same spot a year later when the Adelpha wrecked in a storm. Now, a dozen years later, I still got the feeling he's hanging around, waiting."

I stopped and rubbed my eyes. The script was terribly hard to read, but I guess I should be happy that any record had surfaced. "According to Isaac, the aptain of the Adelpha died off Race Point, so wouldn't he haunt the lighthouse, if that was close to where he died?"

Rob shrugged. "Can't say I've read a lot about ghosts or their habits. Maybe they can go where they want?"

"They tend to stay close to what's familiar, or the source of their demise." I gasped as a thought struck. "My camera didn't work when I tried to take pictures of Race Point lighthouse."

"Probably operator error," Rob teased.

"I took pictures all over the place and of everything—flowers, ocean and beach, people. The only two times it didn't work were at Race Point."

"That is weird, but we've heard the noise here at the cottage and found the crow's nest here. How could that be connected to Race Point?"

I didn't know, but I was excited at the prospect of finding out. I flipped through the next couple of pages until all I saw were blanks. His entries didn't even fill up half the book. "This is the last entry. He certainly didn't write much."

"A man of few words. Maybe he had one of those fishwives who was always yelling and hollering. I bet he spent lots of time up in the cupola just to get away from Maude."

"He loved her. That's why he built the cottage for her."

"And added a ghost to keep her company?"

"I doubt Isaac had anything to do with the ghost coming here. If it is the captain, he seems to be a strong force." I started to read again.

"'Maude don't like the idea of me painting a picture of the captain. Said he was an evil man and deserved to die. I cain't bring me self to tell her about how tortured the captain be. His crew mutinied, but he had his reasons—good reasons—for being so rough. Glad I am the ship was wrecked and most of the remains sank to the bottom of the ocean. The captain were an honest man, if hard, and he prob'ly writ about the happenings in the ship's log. With the captain dead, let the truth and ugliness die with him.'"

"Wow," I said. "Sounds like Captain Aberdeen was a real great guy."

"Whatever happened, the first mate didn't seem to think it was his fault. Did he say anything else about the picture he was painting?"

I turned back to the book, scanning the next couple of pages. "These are water soaked, but I get the gist that he decided to build the trap door and some secret compartments upstairs for the captain to hide treasure in." I scowled. "He knows the captain is dead."

I continued on. *"Captain says a storm is coming and to secure the bridge. I obey then climb the riggin' to the crow's nest. Jimmy ain't much good in storms, and the main mast sways something fierce in the winds. Gotta keep a lookout for pirates, though Captain thinks they're already aboard.'"*

I looked at Rob. "What do you think?"

"Whoever this Isaac is, he's started to hallucinate. If the dates he writes are accurate, Captain has been dead almost twelve years. It was a year after the mutiny when the ship wrecked, dumping Isaac on the shore at Race Point. Maybe he's the one who's haunting the place. Maybe he died of dementia and is wandering around upstairs confused about where he belongs."

I shivered. I didn't want a mad man haunting me, and yet... "Whoever is here, he's not mad or confused. Remember, he saved my life."

I looked down at the last entry, dated 1901. *"'Captain says he'll protect me Maude after I'm gone. He likes the portrait I done of him, but Maude don't. Fooled her though, 'cause I painted it right on the door so as she cain't take it down. Only ways I could see ta have Captain keep her safe. Captain says as how I need to be up on lookout tonight when the moon's full 'cause that be when we might be attacked. Have to hide the treasure first. If the worse happens, Captain says it best go down with the ship as to let those thievin', mutinous pirates have it back.'"*

I leaned back in my chair, astonished by what I read and trying to make sense of it. Rob got up and I heard him banging around in the hall. I rose to follow, coming around the corner and saying, "Don't think about taking this place apart, Rob, to find treasure. Isaac was clearly crazy if he was talking to Captain Aberdeen at the end of his life."

"That's not what I'm doing." He was at the end of the hall with the door to the loft propped open. He pried away one side of the heavy frame that surrounded the portrait. "Look, he really did paint right on the door."

I eyeballed the door where he had removed the frame. There was no canvas beneath; just wood. Now that I really looked closely, I could see from the painting that it was more textured than it would have been on paper or canvas. Textured as in wood grained.

I stepped back, critically eyeing the painting. "So, this is Seamus Aberdeen. This just adds credence to the fact he's here, haunting the place. It's his ship's crow's nest; this is his portrait; and his first mate built the house. I just can't figure out how he got here from where he died and why." Even when there wasn't a storm in the area, the portrait's eyes were scary, like the Captain actually watched us. I stepped close to Rob and wrapped an arm around his waist.

"Why is he still here? He swore he'd see his crew dead for the mutiny, and heaven knows with over a hundred years passing, they certainly are. So why is he still haunting the place? Wouldn't his reason for hanging around be gone?"

So many questions raced through my mind about the journal that I couldn't sleep. Long after Rob softly snored, I sat downstairs making a list of what I needed to research. Now that I had the name of the person who built the cottage—Isaac Shoemaker—I could trace that history as well. I had an idea for a story, but until I had more information, I wouldn't tell Rob. Besides, I had decided it would be a surprise—my gift to him.

When I first started serious writing, it had been as a way of giving something of myself to my family and friends. I didn't do cross stitch like my sister-in-law or make beautiful quilts like my sister. My creativity lay in words—poetry, short stories, novels— not something you could frame and hang on the wall or display on a bed or couch, but it was what I did.

And I realized I was proud of that. Regardless of the fact my ex-husband hadn't found my endeavors to his liking, he had no right to tell me what to write or who should read it. I found joy in putting words to paper in a way that a story emerged, and the characters came alive. Sometimes adventurous and sexy; sometimes introspective and revealing. And always with a little piece of me somewhere in the telling.

I finally crawled back into bed in the wee hours of the morning, mentally drained from all I had discovered and all I needed yet to find.

"Hey," Rob muttered sleepily when I tugged on the covers he laid on.

"Shh, go back to sleep." I kissed his shoulder as I curled against his back, wrapping an arm around his middle and hugging. He laced his fingers with mine and squeezed lightly.

"You're an incredible woman, Bonnie Jo Keeler."

I smiled in the dark. I was finally realizing that. And it felt damned good.

* * *

I spent days in the archives of the local historical society, and again lugged out the tome on the History of Barnstable County. This time I had names as I read through the genealogical records. Once I found Isaac and Maude Shoemaker, I also discovered that

Maude remarried after poor Isaac died, and...

"Oh, no, do not tell me that was her new last name." I swore softly under my breath when I saw the name Norman following Maude Shoemaker. I flipped and scanned, following the Norman name through the rest of the record. I groaned. The records didn't go up to the current day, but there was only one person with the last name of Norman that I knew in Provincetown—Henrietta Norman of the HN Realty Company. Given the size of Provincetown and the number of people that Rob indicated were born and raised here as versus the washashores, and the fact she actually did own the cottage, and I wondered. What were the odds that my nemesis was related to Maude?

There was only one way to find out.

I hoped Henrietta would be out to lunch when I stopped, thinking I could just leave her a note and she might call, or not. She was much easier to deal with over the phone. No such luck. She sat at her desk, immediately narrowing her gaze when I walked through the door.

"I'm not fixing anything else at that cottage for you, young lady. I've spent everything you gave me and then some."

"Actually, I just came for information today, if you have the time." It suddenly dawned on me that if I told her about finding Isaac's book, she might claim it as hers. Rightfully it was, but not until I got done with it. "I've been doing some research on the cottage and think I have an idea of who's haunting it."

She threw back her shoulders and gave me a haughty look. "Who said it was haunted?"

"Isn't that why you didn't want to rent it to me? That all the previous renters wanted their money back because it was haunted?"

"Well, I already told you there's no refund. Besides, your three months are about up."

We were getting off track, and she didn't need to remind me I had little time left before making a decision about the rest of my life. Actually, that decision was ninety-nine percent made, even if I hadn't acknowledged it to the one person I already should have.

I shook my head to clear it. "Do you know of an Isaac Shoemaker?" From the surprised, then horrified look on her face, I hit pay dirt.

"That crazy old man? I'm not related to him, you know.

My great-grandmother remarried before she had children."

"Why do you say he's crazy?"

Henrietta sighed in defeat. "You're just not going to let things be, are you?"

I smiled. "I'm a writer. I love research, and odd and unique characters. I can't help myself. So is Isaac haunting the cottage?"

"It's been so long. I used to go out there when my great-grandmother still lived in it. I was just a little girl, and it was probably my imagination, but I would swear I heard thumping sounds, especially during a storm."

"Did you ever go up into the cupola?"

She looked at me like I was the crazy one. "That thing on the roof? That's just for decoration. In fact, Granny Maude said there wasn't anything past the black curtain at the end of the hall."

"Where the portrait was?"

She nodded. "Granny Maude outlived three husbands and two sons, and it wasn't until my daddy died that the house came to me. And every time I was ever in that house, the curtain was always there. The first time I went out there as owner, I discovered the portrait, and the whole upstairs."

"Do you know who the portrait is of?"

She shook her head. "I have no idea. Some of the family said it was that crazy first husband of hers, Isaac Shoemaker."

"We're back to that again. Why do you say he was crazy?"

She grinned. "I should have stopped talking a couple of minutes ago, huh?"

This time I nodded. Henrietta wasn't so bad, once a person got to know her. She was just afraid some of her ancestor's bad blood had gotten into her veins. Couldn't blame her for that.

"Granny Maude never said much, and all I've got is hearsay passed down through the generations. Seems that old Isaac thought himself a fisherman and talked to some sea captain that Granny Maude said never existed. I guess he's the one who built the cupola on the roof and told Granny it was a crow's nest to keep a lookout for pirates." She laughed out loud. "Isn't that the craziest thing you ever heard—he thought the house was a ship?"

"That does sound kind of nutty," I replied. Apparently Henrietta had no idea that a false door made up part of a wall in the loft, or what lay behind it. Was I committing fraud by not telling her? It was her house, and I was just renting. A fact I intended to rectify.

"Have you thought about my offer? I've decided to stay in the area and have grown accustomed to the cottage."

She narrowed her gaze. "You really are serious about buying it? You haven't had any strange things happen there?"

I gave her my most innocent look as I slowly shook my head. "It's an incredible source of inspiration."

* * *

It's fantastic how much information one can find on the internet. Although most is reliable, it usually still helps for it to be verified. That's why, after a few more days surfing on Rob's office computer, I had reason to believe I needed to go to New York.

"Come on, BJ, you can't go hiking off to every corner of the globe in search of Seamus Aberdeen's ancestors, especially when you don't know if they really are." Rob's argument was valid, but I had talked to this particular man on the phone already, and I honestly thought I had struck gold.

"Rob, the man's name is Seamus Aberdeen Tucker, and he said he was named after an old relative. Do you know how many Seamus Aberdeen's there are listed on any internet genealogy source I looked at?"

He narrowed his gaze. "No, but I suppose you're going to all of them?"

"Nope, just one, because there are only two listed, and the first one we already know is dead. Believe it or not, Captain Seamus Aberdeen of the Adelpha has a mention on a webpage, but only with what we already know. Maritime journals state the ship, the Adelpha, wrecked off the coast in 1890. Since it wasn't a cargo carrying ship or a pirate vessel, it's never been the source of any underwater salvage. There wasn't even any mention of a mutiny."

Rob sighed. "It's really not going to do me any good to argue, is it? Do I have to worry about you running off with this other man?"

I laughed and gave him a hug. "What could an eighty year old man possibly have that I need?"

Rob looked a little less disgruntled when I said that but pouted just the same. "The answers to your questions."

It made me feel all warm and fuzzy inside to know that he cared and maybe was just a little worried. I knew I couldn't leave without giving him a hint of what I was now thinking constantly. "That may be, Robert Garrett, but you are the answer to my dreams."

Chapter 12
The Captain's Story

The address I had been given led me to a high rise condo in downtown New York City. The doorman took my card and scrutinized it carefully before buzzing upstairs and speaking with deference into the intercom. When at last he let me into the building, I was escorted to the elevators, up to the penthouse suite, and then down a long, red carpeted hallway to the door. Whoever Mr. Tucker was, he garnered great respect from those around him. At first I thought it was the wealth, evident in the beautiful paintings on the walls and the plush carpet beneath my feet, but Seamus Aberdeen Tucker proved to be a delightful elderly gentleman.

"Come in, come in," he greeted me at the door. Very tall and straight backed for a man of his years, he had a head full of snowy white hair. His eyes were as blue as the Cape Cod sky, and his smile was enough to capture many a heart even today.

I offered my hand, and he elegantly lifted it to his lips and kissed it. I was flattered and flabbergasted. His gallantry wasn't easily found in today's world, although I must say Rob came very close. He had never kissed my hand, but he was a true gentleman in every sense of the word.

"Mr. Tucker, thank you so much for seeing me. I'm sorry for such short notice."

He waved away my apology. "I love having company and I think, from our phone conversation, your visit will be a delight. But I insist you call me Seamus; or Captain." He chuckled. He led me through a large entry into a sunny living room. Floor to ceiling windows faced the Hudson River and I was struck by the view. From this height, the water looked blue-green, and boats of every size dotted the surface, although they all looked like toys from here.

His living room had a nautical theme with huge paintings of sailing vessels on the walls and a scale model ship on a coffee table. There were barometer and temperature instruments imbedded in a small ship's wheel above the fireplace.

"It's not just the name I inherited from my great, great uncle that explains what you see here. My father was in shipping, and I have always had an affinity for the sea," he said when he saw me continuously gazing from one object to the other. "My parents emigrated here from Portugal in the twenties, and my father was very fortunate to invest in shipping ventures. It was a good life, and now my sons manage Adelpha Shipping."

I looked at him in surprise. "That never popped up on my internet searches," I murmured, but then I had been concentrating on his name and not the name of the ship.

"I can remember as a boy when I learned I had been named after a sea captain, I would pretend to be him; except I was a pirate and looted like Robin Hood. I had a tree house, and it would be my ship."

"Did you ever try to find out more about him? Were there letters or your great-grandmother's journal?"

He chuckled but shook his head. "Ah, the writer emerges. You want concrete evidence of what was a legend in my family? I'm afraid all that's left is hearsay."

"Frankly, I'll be very happy with that. I've struck a dead end in my research."

"Why is my great, great uncle of importance to you?"

I wondered if he would think I was crazy if I told him the truth, but I saw little way around it. "I believe he is haunting the cottage I live in at Provincetown, Cape Cod."

He looked at me, his jaw working. Then he looked to the ship painting hanging on the wall, his brow furrowing. "I often wondered if there was more to the story than anyone told. My great-grandmother was still alive when I was a boy, and while she told me I was named after her brother, even then I knew there was more to the story." His gaze came back to me. "What do you know?"

"Not a lot, I'm afraid. We found a journal in a secret compartment in a storage area of the attic." I pulled the old ledger out of my tote. "It doesn't contain a lot of entries, but they're all written by Seamus Aberdeen's first mate, Isaac Shoemaker. And from what I can gather, Isaac was rather nuts toward the end of his life, so I don't even know if what he wrote holds truth. I turned back to the window while he read the journal entries.

Two tugs, looking impossibly tiny from my vantage point, were maneuvering a large freighter through the water. I wondered idly what cargo it held and its destination. I turned back when Seamus spoke.

"Amazing. The captain named his ship after his sister. Seamus was the one who actually named his youngest sister, and the word Adelpha means dear sister in Portuguese?" He traced over the faded words with his finger. "And this Isaac fellow thought the captain was still there?"

I shrugged. "Like I said, according to a descendant of Isaac's wife, the man was crazy."

"But a mutiny; then a shipwreck? My great-grandmother never knew what had become of her brother, Seamus. She thought he had been lost at sea when she was still a child." He stood suddenly, as though he needed to pace to gather his thoughts. "I just made a pot of coffee; would you like some? Usually, Amanda is here to look after things like that, but today is her day off."

"I would love a cup. May I help?"

He was already walking to the kitchen, which I could see past the breakfast bar at one end of the living room. "No, enjoy the view. It's not often we get such a clear day here in the city."

He quickly returned with two mugs of coffee and cream and sugar on a tray. "I don't do the coffee cups and saucers like my wife. I prefer the sturdier mug. I hope you don't mind."

I smiled. "My cupboard is full of mugs." I took a sip of the hot brew. "How did you come to be named after a great, great uncle? I would think you would be named after your father or grandfather."

"My great-grandmother thought the world of her brother, but unfortunately, she only had girl children." He smiled ruefully. "Seamus isn't exactly a little girl's name."

"No."

"Then my grandmother, Cybil, had only a daughter, Catarina, my mother. If my mother had managed to have my younger brother first, I would have been named John Henry Tucker after my father instead."

I wondered if I would be able to keep all this straight. "But if your brother had been the one named Seamus, I would be talking to him."

He chuckled. "I guess that would be right."

"Why was there such a driving need to carry on the name?"

"The Portuguese are a very proud people and very close knit. When my mother married and came to the United States with her husband, my grandmother and great-grandmother came with them. My grandmother remarried after she came here, so my great-grandmother lived with us for a number of years."

"You have longevity in your family?"

"Adelpha lived to be over a hundred, although we were never quite sure exactly how far over." He put down his coffee mug. "Now, though you showed me Isaac's journal, and told me he thought the captain was still around, why do you think Seamus Aberdeen is haunting the cottage where you live?"

At least he hadn't thrown me out for a quack. "There was a storm and I sleep in the loft of the cottage. During the worst of it, I heard thumping sounds and then I swear someone yelled at me. I raced down the stairs, scared to death. The next day when we surveyed the damage, a tree limb had broken through the roof and landed right in the middle of the bed where I slept. If what I heard was your great, great uncle, he saved my life that night."

He studied me intently. "Have there been other times when you thought you heard something?"

"According to Isaac's journal, there was a mutiny and the captain died, and then a year later the captain's ship, the Adelpha, was wrecked during a storm. I don't know if that has anything to do with it or not but anytime there's a storm, I get treated to loud thumping noises and an even louder 'Yo'."

His smile was evident again. "Yo? As in yo-ho-ho? That sounds very pirate-ish, doesn't it?"

"I understand your skepticism. My friend, Rob, didn't believe it either until he stayed out there one night."

"Ah, and now the plot thickens. Did your ghost cause any more tree limbs to fall on the house, or perhaps on your gentleman friend?"

I scowled. "No, why would you say that? I told you he saved my life." I thought back over the storm when Rob had been at the house. "But, and this is strange, the door to the loft mysteriously locked so we couldn't go to bed." I knew I blushed, because I had called Rob a friend, not a husband.

Seamus was looking thoughtful again. "Perhaps I need to tell you about my great-grandmother's family. Things may make more sense."

"Do you believe your great, great uncle is haunting the cottage?"

"I'm not one to throw cold water on another's beliefs, Miss Keeler, and personally I have never had the opportunity to meet a ghost, but from what you have told me, and what I know about my family, you may very well have Seamus Aberdeen as a house guest." He stood, but turned back to add, "Or would it be the other way around, given he's been there longer? I'll be right back."

He left me pondering his question and thinking of more of my own. In just a minute or two he returned and handed me a small portrait. "Have you ever seen your ghost?"

I started to shake my head but when I gazed at the picture, my mouth dropped open. Piercing dark eyes dominated a face set with a squarish chin and narrow nose. I tilted the picture side to side, and the eyes seemed to follow me. The same way the ones in the door portrait did.

"This is Adelpha, isn't it?"

"Then you have seen your ghost."

"No," I shook my head, "but there's a portrait at the end of the hall—the one Isaac refers to that he painted on the door? Well, it has the same haunting eyes as this picture. Weird." I set the frame down on the coffee table, a shiver racing down my spine. I wished for Rob. He was my anchor and I felt I really needed a reality check about now.

"The portrait is still there, after all these years?"

I nodded. "It's not like it can be taken down and stored in the attic, unless a person wants to remove the entire door." I had a sudden thought. "It might not make any difference to you, but I could get a picture if you want."

"That would be interesting, to say the least."

I quickly called Rob and told him what I wanted. He said he'd go out and take a digital and send it to me, if I had computer access. Seamus nodded when I asked so I told Rob to send it and we'd check email in a bit. As soon as I hung up, I said, "Now it's your turn. You were going to tell me about your family."

He leaned back in his chair, getting comfortable. His eyes closed for just a minute, as though collecting his thoughts, or reaching back for long forgotten memories. "I may not have all the dates right, but it goes back to the 1850's. Seamus was the oldest of several children, born to a poor fishing family. When Adelpha, the youngest of four girls, was born, the father was out to sea and the mother too weak to care for her.

Seamus was only ten, but he took on the task, calling her dear sister, and eventually Adelpha." He shook his head. "Great-grandmother of course has no memory of those times and could only recall that she was about five when Seamus signed on as a cabin boy with a sailing vessel, promising her and her sisters that he would make his fortune and come back and build them a grand house."

"And he never returned for them?"

"Well, she believes he did, but by that time she had been sold to a Scotsman and moved away."

"Sold?"

He nodded. "The times were rough, and her father drank when he wasn't out in a boat, which became the case more and more. He forced her older sisters into prostitution to make his drink money, and one of them was killed by a sailor at the wharf."

"That's barbaric. But sold?"

"You and I might think so, but for my great-grandmother, it was her saving grace. She was a pretty young thing, and when a Scotsman offered her father money to marry her, she was happy to be gone from there."

"How old was she?"

"Only twelve."

"Oh, my gosh. I didn't think things like that really happened." As horrific as the story was, I sat on the edge of my seat waiting for him to continue.

"Adelpha often said her bonny Scotsman was the love of her life because he had given her a life. He had known what happened to her sisters and didn't want the same fate for Adelpha. He couldn't just take her away, so he offered to buy her just to placate her father. But by taking her away from Portugal, she never knew what happened to her brother."

"I thought you said he came back?"

"Years had gone by before Adelpha and her husband traveled back to Portugal because she wanted to see if she could locate what remained of her family. Having a husband to protect her, she didn't fear her father and she worried about her sisters. She found the shack they had lived in torn down by the storms, and one of the local fishermen said her father hadn't been seen in months. But her husband was persistent and finally located one of her sisters.

"According to the sister, who was still a prostitute, their other sister died of the pox, but not before they had both seen their brother, a brawny sea captain with a vessel of his own and, according to my great-grandmother, more gold than Midas."

"Why would her sister have still been a prostitute? Hadn't Seamus come back to build them a fine house and save them from poverty?"

He shook his head. "I don't know. Great-grandmother said she tried to help her sister, but she wouldn't take the money, nor would she go back with her to Scotland."

"Why didn't Seamus track Adelpha down?"

"You have to remember there were no records to speak of back then, especially among the poor. People lived and died without as much as a notice by most folks. The sisters certainly didn't know where Adelpha had gone, and by the time she found her sister and learned of her brother, he was gone again."

I sighed. "That's so sad. No wonder he's still hollering and yelling. He's probably protesting the injustices done to his family over the years."

"Maybe he protected you because he couldn't take care of his sisters," he added to my theory. "Although that doesn't explain why his crew mutinied. There's much to the story of Seamus Aberdeen that may never be discovered."

My phone beeped with a text message from Rob, who said he'd sent the picture. "Our picture has arrived," I said. "You said you have a computer?"

He chuckled. "You say that as though someone my age never heard of such technology. I didn't retire until ten years ago, and we were well into the computer age by then, young lady."

"I meant no disrespect. It just seemed out of place for your décor."

"That's why I have an office." He led the way down a short hall, and I saw another side to Seamus Aberdeen Tucker. Books and papers were piled on every flat surface, including the floor. A very narrow path wove between the stacks and the two of us could barely squeeze behind his desk to view the monitor of the computer.

"Aren't you going to ask what this mess is?" he teased.

I shook my head. "I'm a writer. I know exactly what this is. What are you working on?"

"Shipwrecks on the eastern coast during the nineteenth century."

"And do you have the Adelpha listed as a bit of research?" I sank down into his overstuffed chair and opened my email.

"I didn't have her name. I had tried to trace Seamus's career but there just wasn't anything of significance. But now I certainly will spend some time doing so."

"There." I popped open the picture Rob had sent. "Does he look familiar?"

He looked over my shoulder and I heard him gasp. "It's like looking at a younger version of my great-grandmother; even the shadow of a mustache."

I laughed. "Well, if you decide to come to Cape Cod to research your ship, and if I decide to buy the cottage, you are certainly welcome to the portrait, door and all."

* * *

I caught a cab back to the airport and waited for my flight. I was early but had decided not to use up any more of Mr. Tucker's time although I had enjoyed visiting with him. As I sat in the busy airport, I went over all that he had told me, and I still had questions. Why had the captain turned from a man who wanted to take care of his sisters to a person whose crew mutinied? Was he really a ghost who had protected me because he had failed his sisters?

I pulled Isaac's journal out and opened it, realized it was upside down and started to turn it around. There was writing, beginning on the very first page. I flipped it over to see if I was mistaken; but no, the front had the small, embossed word Ledger on it, and that was the place Rob and I had started. When we came to the end of the entries and found

215

blank pages, I had never even thought about looking clear to the back.

I flipped the journal back over. Opening the back cover, I recognized Isaac's spidery handwriting and began to read, fascinated with the story he had written about his Captain. The story he didn't want anyone to read and with his words, I began to see that he wasn't crazy at all. He was protecting his Captain's reputation; he had his back, just as a good first mate should, and although he had written his story, he hid the journal so no one would know.

I already knew I wanted to write a story about Seamus and his sister Adelpha. On the trip back to Boston, where I'd catch the ferry home, I decided how I would tell Captain Seamus Aberdeen's story. The mutiny occurred because he had cared; not because he was a bad captain. After a hundred sixty years, I realized people needed to know. And then I realized something more important than everything I had learned so far.

I was, indeed, going home.

Chapter 13
Homecoming

As August gave way to September, the air cooled, requiring a sweater to walk the beach in the evening. The sun set earlier so that by the end of September, dark descended before we finished eating most nights. The month was fraught with storms, one after another, as hurricanes pounded the east coast. I had never thought they traveled so far north but I was wrong.

Rob and I spent a couple of days with Freddie and Bob when they came down from New York in late September. They stayed at a beach house in Truro, and we partied and played cards. I enjoyed Freddie's outlook on life. At sixty, he felt he was in his prime, and every day brought new discoveries. Bob was ten years younger, but totally devoted to his partner. At first, I envied them but soon realized I had just such a relationship with Rob. We laughed and talked, sometimes about nothing at all and I could be totally honest with him, about anything. There was no artifice to our relationship, just natural caring of one person for another.

During the worst storms, we soon learned to stay at Rob's house because Captain's shouting and stomping had become almost unbearable. I had concluded he wouldn't hurt me, but I wasn't so sure about his feelings toward Rob. He was a man; and from what I had learned, that made him a threat.

On one occasion at the cottage, I had gone upstairs to change clothes when we got caught in the rain. Since the electricity was still working, I didn't think anything about it until I heard the door click shut behind me. Nothing either of us could do would release it until after the storm passed. From that point on, I didn't go upstairs unless Rob came with me. If we were separated, either he was upstairs or I was and the other downstairs, the door would lock.

Rob kept busy at the bookstore because despite the continuous stormy weather, people were determined to get in their last hurrah on the Cape before winter. I finished my story and submitted it, not telling Rob about the rest of what I found in Isaac's journal. I wanted to surprise him if it was accepted, and I didn't want to have to spill my disappointment if it wasn't.

I now held a copy of Coastal Lore in my hands, hoping that Rob didn't review all the magazines that came to the shop. I nervously opened it to the table of contents to find the page of my story. I had been published in many venues and dozens of times, but for some reason, this was special. It was the first published piece from the new me, the new time in my life. I hoped it measured up.

I rolled my eyes. "Well, of course it does, dummy, otherwise they wouldn't have accepted it for publication." I flipped to the story, which included the picture Rob had taken of the portrait on the door; the only evidence anybody had of Captain Seamus Aberdeen. It was exciting to see my story in print; neat columns that spanned two pages. I started to read, although I knew it by heart, when I heard a car in the drive. Glancing through the front windows, I saw Rob, so I quickly tied a ribbon around the magazine.

Thunder rolled overhead and I groaned. If all went according to plan, I also had a gift for the captain and perhaps it would be the last time I would hear from him. In a way, I would miss his thumping around, but I knew Rob certainly wouldn't. He liked the cottage, which I now owned, and talked about renting his house out and moving in with me.

"Hello," Rob hollered from the back door. We were in the habit of coming in the back rather than the front and I hurried out to the kitchen to greet him, holding the magazine behind my back.

"Hey, yourself." I gave him a kiss, which lingered when he pulled me to him and held me close.

"I love getting greeted like that." He nibbled a path down my neck and my skin heated; just like it always did now that Rob had come into my life.

"I love greeting you like that." I turned his words around. Because of our pasts, we probably worked harder at our relationship, knowing how fragile each other's egos were and wanting to make sure we did it right this time. More likely, I needed to make sure I did it right.

"What have you got?" He felt along my back and snagged the magazine out of my hands. He got a curious expression on his face when he saw the title.

"I wrote the Captain's story, and Coastal Lore published it." I paused, and then added, "It's my gift to you."

A huge grin broke out on his face. "I love presents." He kissed me again, quickly this time, and then released me to look at the magazine. "Congratulations, that's terrific!" He slid the ribbon off and opened it.

"Page one-oh-one," I said, peeking around his side as he opened to the page. I pointed to the bottom of the second page, where I had given him and the Pokey Reader Bookstore credit for my research.

He looked at me with such love, I felt almost embarrassed. "It's just a short story," I stammered, "not a full length book, so I couldn't dedicate it to the love of my life."

I watched his reaction. For a minute, he looked confused, but then his face cleared, and he smiled; that wonderful, you're special smile that told me so much more than words could.

"So, I'm your hero?" He grabbed me and bent me backwards over his arm, taking my mouth in a searing kiss that wouldn't have ended if not for the knock on the door.

"Damn, who's coming out here at this time of night?"

"It's probably Mr. Tucker. I told you he was coming to the Cape to research his great, great uncle and the shipwrecks in the area."

"Tonight?" He scowled. "I was thinking maybe we could celebrate your story."

I left him standing there to go to the front door, used only by guests. "Hi, Mr. Tucker. Welcome to Provincetown," I said as I opened the door.

"I thought you were to call me Seamus," he replied. "It would appear I got here just in time." He stepped into the house just as the heavens opened, the wind pushing rain across the porch.

"I swear there hasn't been this much rain in P'town in many a year," Rob said as he came to stand beside me, sticking out his hand to Seamus. "Hi, I'm Robert Garrett. The Chamber of Commerce is getting mad— bad for tourist business you know."

Seamus laughed. "You may very well have a few more residents now. Some of the folks on the ferry over from Boston swore they wouldn't get on another boat if their lives depended on it."

"Storms do tend to make for choppy seas." Thunder crashed at that moment as though to emphasize my point. I reached out to take Seamus's umbrella and my hand accidentally touched his.

Thump, thump, thump! "Yo! Beware! 'Tis wrong ye all be!" The words echoed through the cottage over the sound of rain pounding the roof.

Seamus's eyes widened and I stepped closer to Rob. The ghostly words had rarely been so clear. What was he trying to tell us now?

"That's him?" Seamus whispered, clearly in awe.

I sighed. "Yep, that's him. I didn't know whether he would say anything tonight. It's not the rain that brings him out all the time. There are other factors."

"Might I see?" Seamus asked.

I looked over at Rob, who answered, "There's really nothing to see. We've never actually seen him. It's just a voice in the dark."

Thump, thump, thump! The boot steps were right above us, louder than I had ever heard them, and from the speed at which they stomped back and forth, more agitated than ever.

"Seamus, do you know something about Adelpha and the Captain that only a descendant would know?"

"What are you getting at, BJ?" Rob asked.

"You haven't had a chance to read the story, Rob, but on the way back from New York, I accidently came across more of Captain's story, in the back of the journal."

He scowled. "You've been holding out on me?"

I gave him a smile and patted his chest. "Only so I could write a story and surprise you with it." When he appeared placated, I continued, "I'm thinking the only way to get the captain to leave is to assure him his sister was happy. Seamus is the only one who can do that, given he's Adelpha's great grandson."

"That makes sense."

"What do we do?" Seamus asked.

"We need to go upstairs," Rob answered. "All of us." He looked directly at me. We knew better than to be separated during a storm, but I had additional reasons because of my research. I needed to protect Rob, and now Seamus, at least until we could get the ghost to accept Seamus's story.

I nodded at Rob. "Okay."

The three of us headed down the hall, but when we got to the portrait, Seamus stopped and stared. "It's larger than life, isn't it? I don't believe my uncle was that tall."

Lightning flashed at that moment and the lights flickered then went out. It had become a pattern Rob and I learned, and tonight he was just as prepared. He pulled the flashlight out of his rear pocket. When he shined the beam of light across the portrait,

Captain's eyes appeared to glow, staring at us with evil intent.

Rob pulled the door open and stood to one side, handing me the flashlight and letting me go first. I stepped across the threshold and turned to find the door closing behind me.

"Rob!"

"Damn!" Rob's hands gripped the front edge of the door, trying to pull it back open. "Grab hold, Seamus. If this door closes, we'll be locked out and Bonnie will be stuck on the side with the ghost."

Another set of hands appeared at the edge of the door and the gap slowly widened. Rob appeared in the space, bracing his back against the doorframe and keeping his arms locked, pushing against the door with all his might.

Thump, thump, thump! "Yo! Beware the devil in man's disguise!"

My heart pounded and my hands shook so hard I could barely keep the light focused. The ghost had never been this riled up. I hoped we were doing the right thing. Did bringing Seamus into the cottage trigger some evil that we hadn't discovered before now?

"Get through," Rob yelled at Seamus, who immediately ducked under Rob's arms and stood beside me on the small landing before the stairs started upward.

"Rob, be careful," I warned, the beam of light wavering as my hands continued to shake. Seamus pushed against the door, hopefully keeping it braced enough so that Rob could slip through.

The second he released his hold and hopped through beside me, the door slammed shut, the walls vibrating with the force of it, the noise echoing in my head. I dropped the flashlight, and it went out, the total darkness reminding me of a tomb. I gasped; afraid I couldn't breathe and would die in the darkness. I began shaking so hard I could hardly stand.

"Hey, honey. It's all right." Rob's arms came around me in the dark and pulled me against his chest. His familiar smell calmed me as I buried my nose in his shirt and just tried to breathe.

"Does this happen on a regular basis?" Seamus sounded surprisingly calm beside us.

I felt Rob shrug, although no one could see it in the dark. "Different things have happened, but he's never been this intent on separating Bonnie and me or been this vocal. We usually just get a Yo." As he talked, Rob ran his hands up and down my back and I gradually calmed.

I tried to remind myself that the ghost wouldn't hurt me. That didn't help when I thought that it might instead do harm to Rob or Seamus, or as thunder kept hammering the air.

"Are we going up, in the dark?" I whispered.

"You can stay down here, and Mr. Tucker and I will go," Rob replied.

"No way. You're not leaving me behind."

"Are you going into the attic then?" Rob asked as he set me away from him. I felt him turn and heard the thunk of his shoe on the first step.

I hated the attic area where the cupola was located. It was always freezing cold to me, although Rob said he never felt it. I had only been up into the cupola once, and that was when we first discovered it and it was daylight.

"The cupola is the crow's nest, above the attic; is that right?" Seamus asked.

I held onto Rob's belt with one hand as he made his way up the stairs. I cautiously put one foot in front of the other, my hand sliding along the stairway wall. I could hear Seamus right behind me. Damn, it was dark.

"That's right," Rob replied. I was too scared to talk.

We reached the top of the stairs, and only through memory could I find my way to the bed. I crawled across the covers and huddled against the wall. When lightning flashed again, it lit the room with a bluish glow, and I could see Rob and Seamus slowly making their way to the secret door.

"Rob?"

"Yeh, honey."

I almost asked him to stop, and we would all go downstairs again. But this had to be finished. And Seamus had come all this way to help. So instead, I sucked it up and tried to be brave.

"Be careful."

I could hear Rob's chuckle across the dark space. "Always. There's too much waiting for me."

Without being able to see, my sense of hearing heightened. The squeak of the hinges as Rob opened the door to the attic grated across my nerves. I strained to see, almost wishing lightning would strike again so I could track their progress.

Thump, thump, thump!

No words followed the heavy drum of footsteps, and I held my breath.

Thump, thump, thump! Louder this time.

I felt lightheaded; realized I was holding my breath and sucked in air. A cold breeze skirted across my skin, and I grabbed the comforter, pulling it up under my chin to protect myself. I tried not to think that a cotton blanket held little protection from a ghost.

Lightning streaked across the sky at that moment, and I could see Rob had left the attic door open. I couldn't see beyond that but heard murmuring. Were they talking to the ghost? Was he replying?

A horrific crash had me jumping off the bed and heading toward the attic before I even realized it. "Rob!" I yelled. I stopped, my hand finding the dresser that sat against one wall and I tried to remember if there was anything in it I could use as a weapon.

I screamed when a hand touched my arm, but then was quickly enveloped in a warm embrace.

"Hey, hang on," Rob said against my ear.

"What was that crash?"

"I pulled the ladder to the cupola down and Seamus climbed up. When I started after him, the whole ladder somehow came unhinged and fell to the floor."

"He's stranded up there?" I squeaked. "With the ghost?"

Thump, thump, thump! This time not only did the footsteps sound farther away, they were much less intense than they had been.

"Where are those candles you keep up here for..." Rob was making little patting noises across the top of my dresser. "Aha." I heard a match strike and slowly the darkness receded as Rob lit two of the fat candles I had on the dresser. He handed me the matches. "Get the ones by the bed."

I quickly lit two more candles that were on the nightstands by the bed, and then hurried back to where Rob stood. I had bought the candles to set a romantic mood, but now their eerie, flickering light seemed to add to the already spooky atmosphere.

"How are we going to get Seamus down?" I hadn't heard a sound from above for long minutes and the worry about Seamus replaced my earlier fear.

"The roof isn't that far above the attic floor. While I could never pull myself up through the hole to the crow's nest, it shouldn't be too hard to drop back through the opening."

"Rob, Seamus is eighty years old. You can't expect him to—"

My protest was interrupted by a thump, followed by a sigh. I peeked around Rob to see Seamus coming out of the attic.

"That was astonishing," he exclaimed with a huge grin.

I was suddenly very angry. I pushed against Rob and stood there, watching the two men as they patted each other on the back, grinning like hyenas, all smiles because of their adventure.

"You two scared me to death," I hollered, and then began to cry. I hated to cry, and it hadn't happened in a long time now, but the fear that had held me in its grip left so suddenly, I didn't know how to react.

"Shh," Rob whispered as he pulled me close. Over the top of my head, I could hear him tell Seamus, "She gets a little emotional at times." I pinched his side. "But she rarely cries," he added quickly.

"Can we get out of here now?" I asked.

The place blazed with sudden light. When my eyes adjusted, Seamus was standing by the top of the stairs, hand on the light switch. He was nodding. "I wondered if the electricity would come back on now."

He appeared to have a grasp on what happened and didn't seem the least fazed by it. Rob blew out the candles and followed me down the stairs. The door opened easily beneath his hand. Seamus turned when the door closed and studied the portrait.

"It's not a very good likeness, although the eyes are certainly my great-grandmother's. The captain was much more rotund and quite a bit shorter than that."

"I thought you didn't have any pictures of him," I replied.

"Oh, I don't," he said, looking from me back to the portrait, "but he certainly didn't look like that when I talked to him just now." He turned and walked down the hall, leaving Rob and me staring after him.

Chapter 14
The Treasure

After I recovered from Seamus's shocking statement about seeing his great, great uncle, I refused to let him leave the cottage until he told all. The rain had lessened to a gentle drizzle, but I warned him the road would be treacherous. Besides, I had made chili and home-made bread.

He gratefully accepted my somewhat threatening invitation, and then returned the favor by refusing to tell us anything until after we ate.

"I will be forever grateful that you found me and gave me a chance to help my great, great uncle." Seamus patted his lips with a napkin before setting it beside his empty plate. "I think he may be at peace now."

"What happened up there; after the ladder fell down?" Rob asked as he poured the after dinner coffee.

"The blowing wind made it feel as though the whole house swayed," Seamus mused. "I felt my chest squeezed, like in a vise, and thought if the captain were there, he was trying to kill me."

"What do you mean, if he were there? I thought you saw him."

"In the dark, with the trees whipping about and shadows everywhere, I thought I did, too." He shrugged. "Now, I'm not so sure. Perhaps I just wanted to see him."

Rob sat back down at the table. "So, your chest got squeezed; then what?" He was more anxious than I to hear the rest of the story.

"I yelled out Adelpha, and then said my name was Seamus Aberdeen Tucker and that I was Adelpha's great grandson." He looked at me. "We don't know what sets the old ghost off, but I told him Adelpha had been happy all her life. I hoped if he knew that, he wouldn't throw me off the roof." He chuckled. "I don't know anything about ghosts, but I swore I actually felt his presence; felt the pressure of his arms around my chest." He took a sip of coffee. "There's not much that can get to me at my age, but that certainly did."

"So, he never really talked to you."

Seamus shook his head. "I guess Isaac's mention of a treasure was just the ramblings of a crazy old man."

"Treasure?" Rob asked, glancing between the two of us. "Did I know about a treasure?"

"Remember in the ledger, Isaac said Captain told him to hide the treasure?" I reminded him.

"Oh, yeah, that."

Seamus looked thoughtful. "I'd like to send in a salvage team," he said, "since I now know where the Adelpha went down. It's not that I believe there was any treasure on board. After all it was a fishing vessel, not a cargo ship. Perhaps it's just that I need to have some closure."

There was a pause in the conversation as everyone thought about all we had learned.

"So now what? Do you think the captain's gone?" Seamus asked.

I shrugged. "He usually only appears on the nights we have storms, and then only during the worst of it. We won't know until another storm comes through." I gave him a grin and a wink. "Rob loves the adventure of it, so you're welcome to come out again and join him."

* * *

"Wow." Rob closed the magazine and let it drop to his chest. He rolled his head to the side and looked at me.

I had been lying beside him in bed, anxiously waiting for him to finish the captain's story and now I nervously bit my bottom lip, watching his face for some reaction.

"You certainly have a way with words, Miss Author Lady. If I didn't know the background, I wouldn't be able to tell the fact from the fiction. Did Isaac's journal tell you about the mutiny?"

"Not exactly, but he gave me enough to make an educated guess. I think Captain Aberdeen was so upset to find his sisters in trade and beyond his help, that he refused his sailors shore leave, knowing they would visit local prostitutes. It might not make sense to us, but I believe he thought he could protect other women against the sailors since he had failed his sisters. In the same way he tried to keep you and me separated."

"That would definitely cause a mutiny." Rob scowled. "But how could the captain cause the shipwreck? He was already dead a year."

I nodded. "The mutiny and the shipwreck happened at Race Point. I think the captain haunted Race Point and when the storm came he caused the light to malfunction, which left the sailors hapless to find their way past the reefs."

"Isn't that stretching it a little?"

I shrugged. "Maybe but remember that my camera didn't work at Race Point either. I think the captain made that happen, too, so I would get involved and tell his story."

Rob laughed, rolling to his side and looping an arm over my waist. "You wrote a terrific ghost story, full of great description and a bit of lore, but except for you and me, and maybe Seamus Tucker, who's going to believe it's anything other than fiction?"

"Terrific, huh?" I smiled at his praise for my writing.

"Yeah, amazingly terrific." He kissed my nose. "I had a thought, though. If Seamus managed to get the captain to leave, you've let a perfect entrepreneurial opportunity slip through your fingers."

"How so?"

"We could have offered ghost tours of the cottage and the cupola; could have even charged double during a storm...or if some girl wanted her boyfriend trapped." He chuckled.

I just shook my head ever amazed at the way his mind tracked. "But we couldn't have lived here for that very reason, remember?"

"There is that," he admitted with a sigh. He pulled me half on top of him and I braced my hands on either side of his head.

I had come to Cape Cod looking for a refuge where I could hide, lick my wounds, and try to find myself. Rob had refused to let me wallow in self-pity, and he offered so much more than I ever thought to have again.

Now, as I gazed into pewter eyes full of love, I knew I had enough to give back. Still, I had to know he was willing to take me as I was and not change me to fit some image in his mind.

"I'm not a morning person, you know." Honesty had always been our hallmark; that would never change.

He grinned. "If you're trying to convince me to hang around, that's not the way to go about it. You're supposed to spout off your good qualities."

I rolled over, resting my head on his stomach. Rob had a nice body—not all hard and packed with muscles, yet not flabby either, but nicely soft and very comfortable. "I'm just telling it like it is. You said change was continual but changing me into a morning person is one thing that will never happen." I stretched my arms out and drew an imaginary heart in the air with my hands. "And I love to write sexy, steamy romance novels."

He reached up and grabbed my hands, tugging me around to face him again. "Now you have it right. I happen to love reading sexy romance novels. Do you think I could be the hero in one of them?" He wiggled his brows.

I laughed. "You are certainly at the heart of the one I'm working on now."

The End

Also by Barbara Baldwin from BWL Publishing Inc.

Dreamcatcher
Loving Charlie Forever
An Interlude
Hold On To The Past
Spinning Through Time
A Game of Love
Always Believe
Tenderhearted Cowboy
Prospecting for Love
If Wishes Were Magic
Love in Disguise
Prelude and Promises

Barbara resides in the Midwest United States but she loves to travel and explore new places, which usually means each of her novels is set in a different locale. She has been published in formats from poetry and short stories to full-length fiction. She really loves writing romance, whether it is contemporary, historical or time travel. She has an MA in Communication and has taught every grade from Kindergarten to college. Visit her website at http://www.authorsden.com/barbarajbaldwin.